HARRY MOON

Snow Day

by
Mark Andrew Poe

Illustrations by Christina Weidman

rabbit publishers

Snow Day (Harry Moon)
by Mark Andrew Poe
© Copyright 2018 by Mark Andrew Poe. All rights reserved.

Rabbit Publishers
1624 W. Northwest Highway
Arlington Heights, IL 60004

Illustrations by Christina Weidman
Cover design by Megan Black
Interior design by Lewis Design & Marketing
Creative Consultants: David Kirkpatrick, Thom Black, and Paul Lewis

ISBN: 978-1-943785-41-4

10 9 8 7 6 5 4 3 2 1

1. Fiction - Action and Adventure 2. Children's Fiction
First Color Edition
Printed in U.S.A.

I'm always close. Although you can't see me, I'm there.

~ Rabbit

Table of Contents

PROLOGUE

Halloween visited the little town of Sleepy Hollow and never left.

Many moons ago, a sly and evil mayor found the powers of darkness helpful in building Sleepy Hollow into "Spooky Town," one of the country's most celebrated attractions. Now, years later, a young eighth-grade magician, Harry Moon, is chosen by the powers of light to do battle against the mayor and his evil consorts.

Welcome to the world of of Harry Moon. Darkness may have found a home in Sleepy Hollow, but if young Harry has anything to say about it, darkness will not be staying.

Family, Friends & Foes

Harry Moon

Harry is the thirteen-year-old hero of Sleepy Hollow. He is a gifted magician who is learning to use his abilities and understand what it means to possess the real magic.

An unlikely hero, Harry is shorter than his classmates and has a shock of inky, black hair. He loves his family and his town. Along with his friend Rabbit, Harry is determined to bring Sleepy Hollow back to its true and wholesome glory.

Rabbit

Now you see him. Now you don't. Rabbit is Harry Moon's friend. Some see him. Most can't.

Rabbit is a large, black-and-white, lop-eared Harlequin rabbit. As Harry has discovered, having a friend like Rabbit has its consequences. Never stingy with advice and counsel, Rabbit always has Harry's back as Harry battles the evil that has overtaken Sleepy Hollow.

Honey Moon

She's a ten-year-old, sassy spitfire. And she's Harry's little sister. Honey likes to say she goes where she is needed, and sometimes this takes her into the path of danger.

Honey never gives in and never gives up when it comes to righting a wrong. Honey always looks out for her

friends. Honey does not like that her town has been plunged into a state of eternal Halloween and is even afraid of the evil she feels lurking all around. But if Honey has anything to say about it, evil will not be sticking around.

Samson Dupree

Samson is the enigmatic owner of the Sleepy Hollow Magic Shoppe. He is Harry's mentor and friend. When needed, Samson teaches Harry new tricks and helps him understand his gift of magic.

Samson arranged for Rabbit to become Harry's sidekick and friend. Samson is a timeless, eccentric man who wears purple robes, red slippers, and a gold crown. Sometimes, Samson shows up in mysterious ways. He even appeared to Harry's mother shortly after Harry's birth.

III

Mary Moon

Strong, fair, and spiritual, Mary Moon is Harry and Honey's mother. She is also mother to two-year-old Harvest. Mary is married to John Moon.

Mary is learning to understand Harry and his destiny. So far, she is doing a good job letting Harry and Honey fight life's battles. She's grateful that Rabbit has come alongside to support and counsel her. But like all moms, Mary often finds it difficult to let her children walk their own paths. Mary is a nurse at Sleepy Hollow Hospital.

John Moon

John is the dad. He's a bit of a nerd. He works as an IT professional, and sometimes, he thinks he would love it if his children followed in his footsteps. But he respects that Harry, Honey, and possibly Harvest will need to go their own way. John owns a classic sports car he calls Emma.

Titus Kligore

Titus is the mayor's son. He is a bully of the first degree but also quite conflicted when it comes to Harry. The two have managed to forge a tentative friendship, although Titus will assert his bully strength on Harry from time to time.

Titus is big. He towers over Harry. But in a kind of David vs. Goliath way, Harry has learned which tools are best to counteract Titus's assaults while most of the Sleepy Hollow kids fear him. Titus would probably rather not be a bully, but with a dad like Maximus Kligore, he feels trapped in the role.

Maximus Kligore

The epitome of evil, nastiness, and greed, Maximus Kligore is the mayor of Sleepy Hollow. To bring in the cash, Maximus turned the town into the nightmarish Halloween attraction it is today.

He commissions the evil-tinged celebrations in town. Maximus is planning to take Sleepy Hollow with him to Hell. But will he? He knows Harry Moon is a threat to his dastardly ways, and try as he might, he has yet to rid Harry from his evil plans.

Kligore lives on Folly Farm and owns most of the town, including the town newspaper.

MAY CAUSE DROWSINESS

Folly Farm Road was just like any other road in Sleepy Hollow once night fell. There was not much traffic, and the only sounds to be heard were the whistling of wind through the branches of the trees and the occasional hooting of an owl.

But every now and then, fleeting shadows could be seen creeping along the road. These shadows crept and crawled; they slithered and slunk. They seemed to come out of the forest, which surrounded both sides of the road, like living things out to explore the night.

Mayor Maximus Kligore, who just happened to live in Kligore Mansion slap dab in the middle of Folly Farm Road, often saw these shadows. He knew these shadows well. In fact, he was spying on them right now from the window of his upstairs study. He watched closely as two shadows darted out of the trees, across the road, and directly toward his house.

Most people would be scared of such a sight—locking their doors, jumping in bed, and pulling the covers up tight. But not Mayor Kligore. Instead, he walked downstairs to his front door and greeted the shadows. When he opened the door, the owners of those shadows were stepping up onto his porch.

2

The light that spilled through the open door revealed creatures that were better suited for shadows. The light showed their rather unique and spooky features.

"Oink and Ug," Mayor Kligore said. "Come on in."

The mayor's two most loyal minions followed him inside and closed the door behind them. They still crept along as if they were trying to hide, mainly because they never felt comfortable in the mayor's house. It was a place they respected very much, but a place where they felt like they didn't belong. It was a grand house, elaborately decorated and quite beautiful. There were candles and books everywhere. It always smelled like a mix of a snobby coffee house and the forgotten shelves in the farthest corner of a library. Anyone else that might have the opportunity to step inside the house would probably have never guessed the most evil man in Sleepy Hollow lived there.

Wasting no time with conversation or pleasantries, Mayor Kligore led them up the

3

stairs to the place where he did his business. His study was the largest room in the house, looking out over Folly Farm Road with a spectacular view of most of Sleepy Hollow. As Oink and Ug took their usual seats, the mayor took his own seat behind his enormous desk. Currently, his desk was covered with several books. One massive tome in particular was sitting in the center. It was a book he used every day. Its pages were yellowed, and the spine was well worn and crackling. It was a book that he relied on time and time again to help him keep his rule over Sleepy Hollow.

"Do you have good news?" Mayor Kligore asked his visitors.

"No news, sir," Oink said. "The town is as secure as always—yours for the taking."

"Then what brings you here at such an hour, Oink? It's nearing eleven o'clock, and I still have enchantments to cast over the town."

"Well," Oink said. "Ug and I found something we thought you might like."

"Is that so?" Mayor Kligore asked, clearly very interested. "What is it?"

Oink reached deep into the folds of the red cloak-like garment he was wearing. After some digging, he pulled out a small black cat. It was fluffy, very tiny, and undeniably cute. It licked its lips with a tiny pink tongue and yawned.

Mayor Kligore backed away from his desk at once, as if Oink had pulled out a bomb rather than a cute, cuddly black kitten.

"That's a kitten!" Kligore shouted.

"Yes, sir," Ug said. "We found it out sniffing around the dumpsters behind Burger Heaven, and it was—"

"It's a *kitten!*" the mayor said again.

"Um, yeah, it is," Oink said. "A black kitten. Evil looking thing if you ask me. We thought you might like to have it. I've never seen a cat as black as this one. Surely it's made for evil works."

The kitten meowed lightly. It then playfully batted at a loose string on Oink's robe with paws as soft as clouds. With another little meow, it started to rub itself lovingly against Oink.

The mayor cringed.

"Oink, you idiot! I am severely allergic to those wretched creatures!"

"You are?" Oink asked, surprised.

"Yes, I am! You know this!"

"No, sir . . . I know you're allergic to kiwis, bee stings, and cats."

The mayor slammed his hand down on his desk, clearly frustrated. The book in front of him jumped several inches into the air. "And just what on earth do you think a kitten is?"

"Well, it's a cat. But it's very small."

"Yes," Ug said. "We thought a small one wouldn't be so bad . . ."

"Morons! Get this cat out of here before I have an episode! Get it out *NOW!*"

"Yes, sir," Ug said with his tail tucked between his legs.

"Sorry, sir," Oink said, rushing out of the study like a scolded child. As they left the room, the mayor could hear his employees apologizing to the cat in cute baby voices. It responded in a series of adorable purring noises.

With a deep sigh, Mayor Kligore returned to his desk. He flipped through the book in front of him and went back to work. He did this every night, casting enchantments over the town to keep it all within his greedy grasp—to make sure it would be Halloween forever. There were numerous spells, enchantments, and incantations he used: one for making sure the trees never sprouted fresh green leaves, one to make sure fishing in Scarlett Letter Lake was always terrible, one to cause at least three people to stub their toes or step on stray Legos, one to keep an aura of spookiness in the air, another to—

As he recited his enchantments, his throat began to itch. He tried clearing his throat and realized that he could also feel his eyes starting to water. With a grumble, he stood up from his desk and walked to the bathroom.

That wretched cat. He was already having a reaction from that brief exposure. History had shown him that if he didn't take something soon, it would get very bad. On a few occasions, his eyes had pretty much swollen shut.

This was just one of the many reasons he preferred dogs. What sort of demonic and sick being could possibly like a cat?

In the bathroom, Mayor Kligore located his allergy pills. He took one more than he usually did because this attack had come on so quickly. He swallowed the pills down with some water and headed back to his study. He had a few more enchantments to cast, and they had to be done by midnight, which was just forty short minutes away.

Clearing his throat again and still feeling his allergies flaring up, he continued, referring to his huge book when necessary. He uttered a few more enchantments and realized that he was getting very tired. His eyes seemed to be struggling to stay open, and his mind was starting to get sluggish. It had been a long day but this was coming out of nowhere . . .

The allergy medicine, he thought. *It makes me drowsy sometimes. And I took more than usual. That was stupid . . .*

Fighting to stay awake, he made it through a few more enchantments. The clock on his wall read 11:49. He wasn't quite done, but he'd be able to get through them all if he really pushed through. There were only a few more to get done and—

10   Without even realizing it, Mayor Kligore's head dropped down. His back reclined into the chair, and within a few minutes, small snores filled his study.

The mayor's eyes had fallen shut, and they would not open again until the morning.

Sometime shortly after two in the morning, a series of strange looking clouds drifted into Sleepy Hollow's skies. These clouds were a very light gray in color, and when they blocked out the moon, they seemed to shine in a very strange way. As these clouds rolled in, they seemed to bring very cold air with them. It was the kind of cold air Sleepy Hollow was not used to; the kind that made the grass shiver and the woodland animals dig a little deeper into their holes and burrows.

If anyone had been standing in front of Haunted Hardware at 2:02 a.m. and looked at the big thermometer and weather dial (no one was there, of course, because it was so late), they would have seen that the temperature read fifty-one degrees. At 2:05, it read forty-two. A mere five minutes after that, it had dropped to twenty-nine.

Shortly after that, the first small white flake fell from the sky. It drifted lazily downward like it was in no particular hurry. Overhead, those odd clouds seemed to expand; a few of them even looked like they might burst.

They did no such thing, but they *did* continue to drop those strange white flakes. The flakes danced in a strange way on the cold air and settled on the ground. Within minutes,

11

a dusting of it could be seen in the yards and roads of Sleepy Hollow.

Everything grew quiet as the white stuff fell from the sky and slowly blanketed the town.

For the first time in an impossibly long time, snow was falling in Sleepy Hollow.

WINTER WONDERLAND

When Harry Moon woke up, his thoughts instantly went to the algebra test he had that day. He'd studied well for it, but something about algebra would just not stick for him. So when he got out of bed that morning, he did it slowly and without much pep in his step. Maybe he could at least talk his mom into making her awesome French toast. That would be a great start to the day. Maybe that would help pull him through to the dreaded test.

As Harry got dressed, he shivered. It felt pretty cold in his room. He brightened a bit when he realized this. Maybe he was getting sick. Maybe he wouldn't have to take the algebra test after all. Sure, it would be a bummer to get sick, but if Harry had to choose between the flu or a math test, well, bring on the fever!

He shook his head, disappointed at himself. He was supposed to be some great magician. He had saved Sleepy Hollow from the clutches of evil countless times, and here he was, terrified of a math test. He knew it was silly, but he just couldn't help it. He sometimes wished there was magic to help him ace algebra tests. Actually, there probably *were* spells like that, but that would be the Bad Magic. And Harry steered as far away from the Bad Magic as he could.

Harry finished dressing and made his bed. As he pulled the last sheet up, he was delighted to find that he did smell something rather French toast-like wafting upstairs from the kitchen. Feeling a bit more hopeful about the day, he left his room and started down the hallway.

On his way out, he was nearly knocked down by Honey Moon, his sister. She was flying down the hall, running faster than Harry had ever seen her move. As Harry pressed himself hard against the wall to let her pass, he watched as she almost missed the stairs because she was running so fast.

"Honey, watch it!" Harry shouted.

"But, Harry, did you see?"

"See what?" he asked.

But Honey had already made it downstairs. Curious, Harry followed after her. He didn't run nearly as quickly as Honey had, but he moved down the stairs with more speed than usual. It was easy when he was being lured by the

15

delicious aroma of Mary Moon's French toast.

When he got to the kitchen, Honey was nowhere to be seen. His dad, John Moon, was sitting at the table, eating a plateful of French toast. His two-year-old brother, Harvest, was sitting in his high chair. He was tearing a piece of the toast in half with a huge smile on his face and sticky syrup on his hands. His mom was at the stove, flipping a piece of toast in a pan.

"What's gotten into Honey?" Harry asked.

"Did you not look out of your window this morning?" Mary asked.

"No . . . " Harry said.

John and Mary Moon smiled at their son. John nodded toward the kitchen window with a knowing grin on his face.

Now more curious than ever, Harry walked to the sink and looked out through the window over the kitchen counter. At first, his eyes refused to believe what they saw. It simply made no sense. What was all of that white? Where had the world gone? What was happening?

"Is that . . . snow?" Harry asked.

"Sure is," Mary said.

As Harry looked out of the window, he saw Honey go whizzing by. She was still running incredibly fast, doing a lap around the house. Fresh powder kicked up behind her as she left her footprints in the snow. That's when Harry realized that not only was there snow on the ground, but it was still falling from the sky.

"Can I go out too?" Harry asked. There was a huge amount of excitement building in him, starting at his toes and slowly inching its way to his brain. It grew and grew as he finally started to understand the very strange reality of what had happened.

It had actually snowed in Sleepy Hollow!

"Yes, you can," John said.

"But go upstairs and bundle up," Mary added. "Get that old parka out of the back of your closet."

With French toast momentarily forgotten and his algebra test just a blip on the radar in the back of his mind, Harry raced back upstairs. As he bundled up, he realized that it had felt so cold when he had changed this morning because it was freezing outside. He dug frantically in his closet to find the parka he'd only worn once and zipped it up as he made his way back downstairs.

When he reached the back door, a thought occurred to him. He turned back to his parents once more before heading out and asked them a very important question.

"So . . . is school cancelled for the day?"

"Yes," Mary said. "It was on the news this morning."

Harry gave an excited fist pump in the air. His algebra test was now no longer a dark rain

cloud hovering over him. It had been obliterated by snow clouds and buried in a world of white.

Harry leapt out of the back door. When he landed in the snow, his eyes went wide with wonder. He was wearing a pair of rain boots

and two pairs of socks, so he didn't feel the coldness right away. And even if he had felt it, he wouldn't have cared. This was snow. Actual real *snow*. He'd seen it on TV and movies and had read about it several times but, in his thirteen years of life, had never experienced it for himself.

He reached down, grabbed a handful, and threw it into the air. Just as it started coming back down, lost in the flakes that were still falling from the sky, Honey came lapping back around the house. She was giggling like a toddler. She spotted Harry, came running at him, and knocked him down in a playful tackle.

They went sprawling into the snow, laughing. Harry gathered up some of it, made his first-ever snowball, and lobbed it at her. It hit her in the butt, and she yipped like a little dog. But she was still laughing. She then made her own snowball and started chasing Harry around the house with it.

Within minutes, Harry's chest was hurting from all of the laughing, and his face was

getting chilled from the cold air and falling snow. After Honey had nailed Harry in the back with her snowball, they fell down together in the snow and waved their arms and legs. They made the perfect shapes of snow angels together as Harry opened his mouth and stuck out his tongue and caught several snowflakes. He almost expected them to taste sweet, but there was no taste at all (but it was cool to feel them melt on his tongue).

This is awesome, Harry thought. *And there's still French toast to look forward to!*

21

In that early morning hour, the Moon's snowed-over front yard was filled with laughter. It was a loud sound of joy that carried a few yards over. The same noise could be heard over much of Sleepy Hollow that morning as children (and some adults) ran outside to explore the snow.

It was the sound of a town enjoying their first winter wonderland in nearly fourteen years.

22

No Time for Snow Time

The television was on in Mayor Kligore's study, and he did not like what he saw. In fact, he was literally fuming at what was on the screen. There was just too much to take in, and with every bit of news he saw,

his anger grew by leaps and bounds.

First, there was the weather map that the weathermen kept showing. The map showed a white arc that swept directly across Sleepy Hollow. The meteorologists were calling it a "totally unpredicted and freak snow storm." They were scratching their heads over it, wondering how their state-of-the-art weather predicting equipment had missed it.

It's because I control the weather here, he thought with a snarl.

But even worse than the idiot weathermen talking about how special and remarkable this snowfall was, there was the strange phrase that the reporters kept saying: *schools closed.*

Those two words together made the mayor cringe.

Apparently, when nine inches of snow fell, schools did not open. Something about hazardous driving conditions for the buses. It was ridiculous. Nine inches of snow outside and

still falling. The folks on the news were smiling and saying how beautiful an unexpected snow storm could be. But all Mayor Kligore could see was failure.

Last night's allergy medicine had knocked him out cold. He'd fallen asleep before he'd been able to recite the enchantment to keep snow out of Sleepy Hollow. It was one of the most important enchantments he had to cast between early November and late March every year. He saved it for last because it was a long enchantment, and it made him think of snow. And he hated snow. No, he *loathed* it. It was too white, too clean. Something about the sight of it made him think of hopes and dreams and frolicking children.

Thinking of it all made him shudder.

He looked out his window to the town below. Here it was, not even nine o'clock in the morning and there were kids gleefully dashing here and there. He saw a group of children sledding down the hill between Mayflower Road and Folly Farm Road. Another handful were

25

building snowmen in one of the yards behind Magic Row.

There was a blanket of whiteness over everything . . . and happiness. Happiness everywhere. A day off from school and the first snowfall in Sleepy Hollow in a very long time.

He knew that it was too late to correct things. The enchantment had not been spoken, and the snow was already here. He could do nothing until tonight's spells and enchantments session. But there had to be something he could do to make up for his mistake, for his failure.

Slowly, an idea crept into his head. A wide grin spread across his face as the idea grew. He looked down to those miserable little brats sledding, building snowmen, and running aimlessly through all that horrible snow. With the evil smile still on his face, he picked up his phone and punched in a number.

Several seconds later, Oink answered on the other end. And before he could so much as say hello, Mayor Kligore said, "Call an emergency meeting, and do it *now*."

Forty minutes later, there were five figures sitting at a large table in an underground chamber beneath Folly Farm known as the Grotto. It was where Mayor Kligore and his We Drive By Night Company usually did its more pressing business. Underground, six hundred and sixty-six feet beneath the snow-covered landscape of Sleepy Hollow, they could do business away from any prying eyes or ears. It was also conveniently located directly beneath the Kligore mansion.

And most importantly, there was not a single flake of snow in sight.

The five in attendance at this emergency meeting were Mayor Kligore, Oink and Ug, his eldest son, Marcus, and his younger son, Titus. Titus looked a little nervous to be in the Grotto. He also kept giving uncertain glances in Oink and Ug's direction. He was only thirteen years old, and while he was destined to follow in his father's footsteps, he was not quite as ready as his brother. Marcus, on the other hand, was chomping at the bit to take his father's place and would do anything asked of him. The only problem he had was pretty girls and fast cars kept distracting him. Still, there was an undeniable evil lurking beneath his typical teenage temptations. It showed in the excited mood he brought to the table. Titus guessed it was something that just came with age.

"Is no one else coming?" Marcus asked.

"No," Mayor Kligore said. "We have no time to arrange for anyone else. For today's agenda, it has to be the four of you."

"Does it have something to do with the snow?" Oink asked.

"Yes, it does," Kligore said, seeming to cringe at the word.

"Did you finally make it snow?" Titus asked.

29

"Absolutely not," Mayor Kligore said. "In fact, it was a mistake on my part. And it's all the fault of that stupid cat!" He stared Oink down with this last word. Oink shifted in his seat and slid down a bit, as if trying to hide.

"Anyway," the mayor continued, "what I need the four of you to do is to stop all of this . . . all of this *fun!*"

"Sounds like an easy job," Marcus said. "What did you have in mind?"

"Oh, I don't know," the mayor said with a

grin. "The children in Sleepy Hollow are having far too much fun out there. And it's my own fault. I admit it. I need the four of you to do me proud—especially you, my boys. Marcus and Titus, go out there and strike some terror into their hearts. Make them *fear* the snow. Do whatever it takes."

"Anything?" Titus asked. He seemed a little uncertain. Maybe even afraid.

"Yes," the mayor said. He then looked around the Grotto suspiciously. He sniffed, cleared his throat, and then sneezed.

"Getting sick, boss?" Ug asked.

Beside him, Oink made a little moaning sound. He seemed to be holding his cloak tightly together.

"No," he said. "It's allergies." He looked at Oink again and said, "Do you still have it?"

"The kitten?" Oink asked, sounding like he was offended at the notion. "Of course not! I know

how allergic you are, and after last night I—"

He was interrupted by a loud purring noise from under his cloak. His eyes went wide, and he stepped away from the table very quickly.

"Oink," the mayor said. "Get out of here with that infernal cat!"

"Sorry, sir," Oink said. "But I couldn't just leave it. It's so small and defenseless, and it likes me!"

31

"I don't care! Get out of here!" Oink and Ug scrambled away from the table and ran for the elevators that would take them back to the snowy grounds of Folly Farm. As they retreated, one final little *meow* could be heard through the cavernous Grotto.

Mayor Kligore turned his attention back to his sons, rubbing lightly at his nose while fighting off a sneeze.

"Marcus, I trust you to keep these three in line. And Titus, this is your chance. Show me what you're made of, son. Help Marcus keep

Oink and Ug in check. Also, most of the kids out there playing are around your age. You think like them, so I expect you to be a huge help to Marcus today. Am I understood?"

"Loud and clear," Marcus said, cracking his knuckles, ready to start.

"Understood," Titus said.

"I've even got some ideas for outfits," Marcus said with a smile.

"Oh, don't get dramatic about it."

"Trust me, Dad," Marcus said. "Give me half an hour, and I'll have the four of us decked out in outfits that'll scare these snow-loving pukes out of their minds."

"Fine. Just get to work. Do me proud, boys!"

He watched as his two sons hurried off and was rather proud of them. He had no doubt that they would fix his mistake. And soon enough, the town of Sleepy Hollow would be praying that it never saw snow again.

SCARY SNOWMEN

With something as monumental as the town's first snow occurring, it did not take long for the members of the Good Mischief Team to get together. Bailey called Harry, Harry called Hao, and Hao called Declan. And soon after, they were in Harry's front yard building a massive snow fort. Snow was flying into the air in plumes as the four boys worked together to create a structure they never thought they'd have the pleasure of making. They worked with the dedication of construction workers as they packed the walls and leveled off the floor.

With four young boys working on it, the fort went up quickly. As they built, Harry realized that his fingers were getting cold. He had on a nice pair of gloves, but snow was getting into them and sliding up into the fingers. His mother had told him that it had not snowed in Sleepy Hollow in nearly fourteen years so the Moon household was rather limited on appropriate snow attire. That's why the gloves were too big, and the parka he'd pulled from the back of his closet had been collecting dust ever since he had received it as a gift from his grandmother four Christmases ago.

Harry pushed past the icy chill of his freezing fingers and carried on. He and Hao were packing in the inner walls of the fort while Bailey and Declan built the outer walls. It was already taller than Harry; he had to stand on his tiptoes to pack in the edge overhead.

For kids that had never had the chance to build a snow fort, Harry thought they had done pretty well.

"So, what do we do after this?" Bailey asked.

"Snowball fight," Declan answered.

35

"Let's build a snowman," Hao offered.

"I vote for sledding," Harry said. "Honey is sledding with some friends. They've got a bunch of sleds. I'm pretty sure they'd let us use them."

"That's good," Declan said. "My folks said they tossed our sleds out years ago since it never snows around here."

"Sledding sounds like a blast," Hao said. "Great idea, Harry."

With the idea of sledding in their heads, the four boys acted quickly to put the finishing touches on their fort. A well-placed right-handed punch from Bailey gave them a spy window. A combination of teamwork and frigid hands gave them an escape tunnel out of the back where they had packed an extra mound of snow. When they were done, they all looked at it with great pride and rosy cheeks.

"Before we go sledding," Harry said, "let's go inside for some hot chocolate. My fingers are starting to go numb."

"Same here," Bailey said. "I stopped feeling my toes about twenty minutes ago."

The four of them left the fort behind and headed for the Moon household. They threw snowballs and kicked up clouds of powder as they went, acting a few years younger than their ages but feeling that it was okay. After all, none of them had ever experienced snow before—not even Declan, who had relatives out in Colorado.

It was new, it was cold, and it was exciting. It was almost like Christmas as far as Harry was concerned.

They were soaked, freezing cold, and their noses were the color of turnips, but it was well worth it. This was one of the very best days any of them could remember, and it could surely only get better.

While four young boys ran into the Moon house to enjoy hot chocolate, four other figures were marching behind the businesses along Magic Row. They were dressed in white hooded sweatshirts and puffy white sweatpants. The hoodies were up over their heads, drawn tight against their skulls. They also wore white ski masks that covered the rest of their faces. The ski masks had been painted to make them look like creepy snowmen—with thin hateful eyes and leering mouths of coal that were stretched into a creepy smile.

They also wore gloves tipped with claws. And

although the claws were made of rubber and could not really hurt anyone, they were still very scary. Because of their white outfits, they were able to make their way through the snow without anyone seeing them. That's why no one noticed them when they crept toward a group of eight kids sledding down one of the biggest hills in town.

The fake snowman in front looked back to the other three. When he spoke through the ski mask, his voice was muffled and deep. Not only did they *look* menacing, but they sounded creepy too.

"Just follow my lead," the snowman said.

The other three nodded in response. They were all smaller than their leader. One of them was barely over three feet tall and had what appeared to be a rat-like tail sneaking out the back of his white pants. It dragged along in the snow behind them, leaving a thin little trail.

The snowmen raced to the hill and ducked down behind a mound of snow. None of the sledding children saw them because they were having too much fun. Together, the snowmen all started to make snowballs—big melon-sized ones and smaller ones as well. They stockpiled them and then waited for the next sledding kid to take their position at the top of the hill.

"Wow, that actually looks like fun," one of the smaller fake snowmen said. This snowman watched the kids sledding down the hill, squealing and laughing the entire time. It was fairly obvious that this showman would rather be sledding than trying to stop the kids from having fun.

"Shut up, Titus," the lead snowman said. "We're not here to have fun. We're here to stop the fun. Now, *attack!*"

With that, the lead snowman got to his feet and started pelting snowballs at a boy no older than eight years of age as he started to take off on his plastic sled.

The first snowball hit the boy in the back just as his sled had started to slide down the

39

hill. When the kid turned around to see what had happened, he caught another one in the face. He went reeling backwards and fell off the sled. When he hit the ground, he went rolling head over feet in a whirlwind of arms and legs. He started to cry before he even reached the bottom of the hill.

By the time the boy reached the bottom of the hill as a kid-shaped snowball, the other kids noticed the four stalking snowmen coming toward them. The snowmen were scary, and they were loaded down with snowballs.

Without warning, the four mean snowmen started to pelt the seven remaining kids. One unfortunate girl caught a snowball to the butt while another one took a large one to the shoulder. And still, the evil snowmen advanced.

Among the crowd was a certain young girl named Honey Moon. When one of the smaller snowmen pegged a snowball at her, she held up her sled as a shield. The snowball struck it hard, driving her backward. It also put a crack directly in the center of the sled, breaking it in half. Honey Moon dropped the two pieces of sled in anger and bent down to start making her own snowball. Beside her, her friend Claire Sinclair was trying to retreat. She caught a snowball to the back and went face first into the snow.

Honey stood up with her snowball and threw it as hard as she could. It missed the lead snowman by a few inches. He turned in her direction and, somehow, threw two snowballs at once. The first missed her, falling just short of her feet. The other hit her in the stomach. She gasped as the breath was knocked out of her. Tears stung her eyes, and she went to her knees, hurt and afraid.

41

She glanced around and saw that all the other kids were on the ground, crawling away. Some were crying. Poor Dougie Vaughan, the kid that had been knocked off his sled and sent rolling down the hill, was walking around down there like he was dizzy or lost.

As the lead snowman got closer to Honey, he picked up a fallen sled from the ground.

42

When he looked at her, Honey understood that these were just creeps in costumes. But still, she was more frightened than she had ever been in her life.

With a small grunt, the lead snowman broke the plastic sled over his knee and threw the broken pieces to the side.

"Go home," the snowman said. "Play time is over. Go back home, and don't even think about coming back out. If you do, you and all of your friends will have to answer to us again!"

Honey hated to back away from such a bully, but she was scared, on the verge of crying, and her stomach was still aching. She turned away before the creeps could see her cry. She helped Claire Sinclair to her feet, and together, they walked toward the street.

43

The lead snowman watched them go. He watched all eight of the kids that he and the other three snowmen had easily frightened off scatter in every direction. Some of them looked back at the evil snowmen with fear and terror.

It made Marcus Kligore smile very widely under his snowman ski mask.

He tightened the hood of his sweatshirt and turned to the other three. "Very nice work," he said. "Now let's see who is next."

And just like that, the four frightening

snowmen seemed to vanish into the still-falling snow just as quickly as they had appeared.

GOOD MISCHIEF TEAM, ASSEMBLE!

B y the time Harry downed his second
cup of hot chocolate, his fingers had
started to feel normal again. The chill

was gone, but he was surprised to find that he sort of wanted it back. Sure, it was cold outside, but that was part of the fun. Harry, Bailey, Declan, and Hao had spent the last fifteen minutes making plans for the rest of the day as the drank mugs of hot cocoa—plans that included many dangerous ideas involving sleds and ramps made of snow.

They were so excited about the plans they had made that they didn't hear the front door open. They didn't even see that Honey had come home in tears until they were putting their empty mugs in the kitchen sink.

It wasn't until they turned to head out of the house that they saw her. She was coming into the kitchen, wet and dropping clumps of snow on the floor. She was crying, tears streaking her reddened face. When Harry saw her, his protective-brother alarms started going off.

"Honey," he said. "Are you okay?"

"No, not at all!" she yelled. "I was out sledding with Claire and some other friends. We

46

were having a blast until these . . . these *evil snowmen* showed up. They beat us up with snowballs and broke the sleds and . . . and . . ."

She trailed off here, crying openly now. She went to one of the kitchen chairs and put her head on the table, still crying. Harry went to her and put an arm around her. Declan went to the cupboard and set to making her a cup of hot cocoa.

"Evil snowmen?" Harry asked. "What did they look like?"

47

That's when another voice filled the kitchen. There was an edge to it that was even braver and sterner than Harry's protective big-brother voice. It was the voice of Mary Moon, concerned for her children. It was probably the strongest voice Harry had ever heard, even more than his dad's when he got upset or angry. He and Honey had come to call it Mary Moon's momma-bear voice.

"Yes, I'd like to know what these *snowmen* looked like," Mary said. "Bullying like that can't be tolerated. Perhaps I should call the police."

"Well, it was just some guys in snowmen costumes," Honey said. "White hoodies, white ski masks, and white pants. Oh, and these really creepy gloves that made them look sort of like a yeti or something."

"Did they hurt you?" Harry asked.

"I got a snowball to the stomach," she said, getting herself together now as the crying tapered off. "Some of the other kids got it worse, though."

"Yes, I think something should be done about this," Mary said, going to the phone.

As Mary Moon called the Sleepy Hollow Police Department, Harry and the rest of the Good Mischief Team gathered around Honey. When Declan came over, he brought a fresh mug of hot coca, which he placed in front of Honey.

"Thanks," she said, taking it with shaking

hands.

"How many were there?" Harry asked.

"Four," Honey answered.

Harry and his pals looked to one another, recognizing right away that there four of them too. They all nodded in unison, making an agreement without saying a single word.

"Oh, Harry," Honey said. "I don't know about that. These guys were really mean. I don't think you should try anything."

"It'll be okay," Harry said, heading upstairs. He looked back at the rest of the Good Mischief Team and said, "Meet me in the front yard in two minutes."

Harry ran upstairs and headed for his room. He grabbed his wand from his desk and put it into his backpack. As Sleepy Hollow's greatest aspiring magician, Harry was aware that there was a huge difference between using his wand for magic shows and using it as a means of defense. Whenever he knew he was taking it into a confrontation, something about it felt different. When he was performing at birthday parties and making kids laugh, the wand felt light to the touch. During those times, fun seemed to radiate off of it. But those other times, when he was taking it as a weapon, it felt heavy and almost dangerous. His wand and the Good Magic he used through it were to be used responsibly. This was exactly what the wand seemed to tell Harry through his book bag as he left his room.

"Hold on, Harry," said a voice from behind him.

Harry recognized the voice right away. He stopped, turned, and saw Rabbit standing on his bed. His large ears were rather droopy, as always. His large feet walked forward on the mattress. Harry wondered how useful those feet might be in the snow.

"Are you sure you want to do this, Harry?" Rabbit asked.

"I think I have to," Harry said. "I know Mom said she's going to call the police to report it, but we both know Mayor Kligore sort of rules the police. So, they probably won't do anything. And, I don't know, Rabbit. Bullies picking on little kids—on *my sister!* I have to do something. Don't I?"

"That's a very brave and noble way to think about it," Rabbit said. "I think it is wise to look into it, yes. But I don't know that you need to draw your wand right away."

Harry thought it over, and although he knew Rabbit was right, the idea of putting a stop to the evil snowmen was too good to ignore. Still, he had learned long ago to always rely on his instincts—instincts that were usually pretty in tune with Rabbit's good advice.

"You're right," Harry said. "I won't use it unless it's absolutely necessary."

"I think that's for the best," Rabbit said.

"Why don't you come out with me?" Harry asked. "I think you'd really like the snow!"

"Oh, I love the snow," Rabbit said, turning his head and peering out of the bedroom window. "So clean and white and pure."

"Well then, come on!"

Rabbit smiled again and hopped down from the bed. He went over to Harry and gazed up at him. "I'm always close," he said. "You know this about me. Although you can't see me, I'm there. Speaking of which, that was a nice fort you boys built earlier."

Harry laughed and gazed down at Rabbit. He sometimes forgot just how special his magical friend was. Rabbit *was* always with him. It was something that Harry had gotten so used to that he wondered if he had started to take it for granted.

With his backpack slung over his shoulders, Harry headed back downstairs where Honey was still sitting at the table with her hot cocoa. He gave her a final look and headed outside, suddenly feeling that there was indeed someone else with him.

He smiled and looked to the snow, fully expecting to see rabbit tracks, but there were none.

❧

They found one sled in the Moon garage and another two at Bailey's house. They could not find a fourth, but Bailey remembered seeing a YouTube video where some kid had used a large baking sheet as a sled. After some begging, he managed to get one from his mother. After that, they were off.

"Explain this to me, Harry," Hao said. "These snowmen attacked Honey and her friends while they were sledding. So why are we going sledding? Seems like we're opening ourselves up to be attacked, doesn't it?"

"Exactly," Harry said. "We could waste a lot of time wandering around town hoping to find them, or we could make them come to us."

"And have some fun in the process," Declan said, banging his sled like a drum.

They did not realize it at the time, but they were walking very fast. Harry knew that Honey had gone sledding behind the street and businesses on Magic Row, but he had another hill in mind. This hill was a massive drop in the land that went all the way down to the intersection of Paul Revere Avenue and

Mayflower Road. There was a running joke at school that had named the hill Haunted Hill because it was believed the hill was so steep that if anyone ever fell down it they would surely die.

Although they were headed that way to try to draw out the bullies in snowmen suits, they also knew that they'd get some sledding in. And for thirteen-year-old boys that had never had the pleasure of tearing down a hill in the snow at breakneck speeds on plastic sleds, the anticipation was just too much.

Even though they could possibly be heading into a dangerous situation, they could not hide their smiles.

As they made their way farther across town, they spotted a large orange truck coming down the road. There was a plow on the front of it, and as the truck crept down the snowy road, the plow went up and down, up and down. The truck itself veered all over the road, from one lane to the next. Something under the hood sputtered and coughed.

"What's that?" Hao asked.

"Snowplow," Declan said. "My dad was telling me about them this morning. Apparently in places where it snows, there's a department in the city that goes through and plows the roads so people can drive. But here in Sleepy Hollow, it's been about fifteen years since it snowed— so the plows are sort of out of shape. Dad said he figured with plows that don't work and plow drivers that don't know what they're doing, we might be out of school for at least three days."

56

The boys cheered at this. The thought of more missed days of school put more speed into their step as they skirted around the town square and neared Paul Revere Avenue.

As they walked along, they passed other kids. Most of them were younger, being escorted by adults. They even passed a group of high schoolers that were running through the snow equipped with sleds and a snowboard. As they walked toward the town square, Harry spotted Mrs. Brewster, the postmaster, trying to maneuver the mail truck through the badly plowed roads. From what Harry could tell, she was having quite a bit of trouble. Other cars had tried making their way into town and were having the same trouble. The vehicles crept along very slowly, inching along carefully. Most people, though, had chosen to stay inside and wait for the roads to clear up before venturing out.

"Guys," Bailey said suddenly. "Look."

He was pointing ahead of them, down the street between Haunted Wood Brasserie and Spook-Tacular Sales. Like everything else, the town ahead of them was covered in snow. Although the flakes had finally stopped falling, the snow had delivered enough powder to nearly come up to the boys' knees in some places.

Straight ahead, Haunted Hill rose up behind the stores. Paul Revere Avenue was nothing more than a faint line among the white, poorly plowed by the snowplow they had seen earlier.

"Whoa," Bailey said.

"Yeah," Harry said. "That looks a little . . . dangerous."

They all looked at one another, smiles slowly blooming on their faces. They broke into laughter at the same time and started running toward Haunted Hill with their sleds (and baking sheet) banging alongside them.

BATTLE ON HAUNTED HILL

arry was winded by the time they reached the top of Haunted Hill. His lungs were burning, and his knees felt like jelly. Walking up the hill in what was easily nine inches of fresh snow had been no easy task, but now that they were at the top and looking down, it was all worth it.

They could see most of the town, all the way to the farthest edge of the town square, from where they stood. Covered in a sheet of white, Sleepy Hollow was a beautiful sight to behold. It looked almost like a different place altogether. More than that, everything was quiet, as if the snow had absorbed all of the usual sounds.

"This is so cool," Declan said, placing his sled on the ground.

It truly was. Harry was fairly certain that what he was seeing would stick with him for the rest of his life—his first snow, covering the town he had grown up in and knew so well. The white sheet sparkled in the lazy sun overhead. It was almost enough to make him forget why they had trudged up to the top of Haunted Hill.

Almost.

A quick game of paper-rock-scissors decided on who would get the baking sheet rather than the plastic sleds. Declan lost but took it in stride. He plopped the baking sheet down onto the snow and sat on it as Harry, Bailey, and

Hao took a seat in their sleds.

Now seated, there was no backing out. The hill was enormous, and for a moment, Harry wondered if this was a mistake. There was a fine line between dangerous and fun, and what they were about to do balanced right along the edge of that line.

"Ready?" Harry asked before he could change his mind.

"Ready!" the other three cheered.

"One," Harry said, starting their countdown. "Two . . . three!"

They each pushed off at the same time. The sound of snow crunching under the sleds was like music to Harry's ears. Right away, his sled started to pick up speed. It was slow at first, but then, as the hill dropped off more and more, the sled moved much faster. At one point, Harry understood that even if he did get scared, bailing off of it could be very dangerous. He was going so fast there was no surefire way to know what would happen.

So, he simply rode it down, hanging on for dear life. His heart was pumping with excitement and fear while his cheeks ached from the wide smile he wore as he rocketed farther down.

Chilly wind blasted his face. The sled kicked up powder that flew out to all sides. The town grew closer and closer, but the ride stretched on. It was then that Harry realized he was smiling. When he felt the smile there, the part of his mind that had been afraid of sledding down Haunted Hill was gone. It was replaced by the absolute thrill of it. It was quite possibly one of the most fun things he had ever done.

He looked to his left and then to his right. His friends were having the same amount of fun, their faces bright and filled with excitement. Harry was shocked to see that Declan was ahead of the pack, the baking sheet blasting down the hill and spitting out a plume of snow behind him. He was yelling a loud cheer as he held on to the edges of the sheet for dear life.

When Harry finally reached the end of the hill and the ground leveled out, he realized that he was still moving along very quickly. With the intersection of Paul Revere Avenue and Mayflower Road just a few feet ahead of him, Harry leaned hard to the right. This caused the sled to turn hard in that direction at a sharp angle. The sled came to a sliding stop, tossing Harry off.

Hao and Bailey did the same, and they all came to a stop just in time to realize that Declan could not steer his baking sheet the same way they steered their sleds. He was rocketing across the ground, headed straight for the road. Fortunately, the snow had kept people off the streets so when he hit the curb and went flying out into the road, there was no traffic. Harry, Hao, and Bailey watched in terrified wonder as Declan struck the curb and went airborne. His butt, along with the baking sheet, went three feet into the air and sailed almost entirely across Mayflower Road. When he landed and was thrown from the sheet, his friends got to their feet and started running in his direction.

Before they got there, Declan was on his feet and laughing hysterically. "That. Was. AWESOME!"

The four boys laughed together in the middle of Mayflower Road, cheering. Their hearts were pumping wildly, and their cheeks were sore from laughing and the bitter cold of their unexpected snow day.

Without verbally agreeing to do so, they all headed back up Haunted Hill to do it again. Halfway up, Harry felt foolish for not having considered the annoying fact that every time they went down the hill, they'd have to walk back up it. His legs were already protesting, but he ignored them, thinking of the next trip down the hill.

The boys were more winded than ever when they reached the top. Harry was sweating and panting for breath. They took a moment to rest and communicated in the way that good friends do—with nothing more than a smile and a nod, all together.

Once again, they sped down Haunted Hill. When they reached the bottom this time, Declan was able to bring his baking sheet to a stop before rocketing out in the street. After a brief rest, they went back up the hill, then back down. And up again and back down again and again.

On their fifth trek back up Haunted Hill, Harry's legs were beyond sore. It was almost painful to walk. He was pretty sure this would be their last climb. Pulling his sled behind him, he crested the top of Haunted Hill and readied his sled for one last trip.

That was when he saw the four walking snowmen.

The snowmen were just to their right, walking slowly toward Harry and the rest of the Good Mischief Team. He saw that Honey had not been exaggerating. Even though they were clearly costumes or outfits of some kind, these snowmen were pretty terrifying.

Harry had gotten so caught up in sledding

65

that he'd forgotten why they had come to Haunted Hill in the first place—to lure out these evil snowmen.

Each of the snowmen was holding a large snowball. One of the figures was much smaller than the others, and Harry was pretty sure he caught a slight movement beneath it. To Harry, it looked like it had been dragging something in the snow but then yanked it back up into its costume.

That was a tail, Harry thought. *A rat's tail. That's Ug!*

He stood his ground as the snowmen approached. Bailey, Declan, and Hao stood by him, dropping their sleds as they slowly went to their knees to make their own snowballs. Harry sized up the other three snowmen and was pretty sure he knew each of their identities. If the smallest one was Ug, he was pretty sure the slightly larger one was Oink. As for the other two, one *had* to be Marcus Kligore. And the fourth was likely Titus.

"Well, well," said the lead snowman, whom Harry assumed was Marcus. "We lucked out on this one. If it isn't the amazing Harry Moon!"

"What do you want?" Bailey asked.

"Oh, just to have some fun of our own," said the lead snowman. Listening to the muffled voice, Harry was now certain that it was Marcus Kligore.

"Fun," Harry said. "So that means you find it fun to bully kids much younger than you?"

"It does, actually," Marcus said.

"You attacked my sister this morning," Harry said.

"Did I?" Marcus said. "I would have never known. All these snotty-nosed brats are so excited about snow today. They all look the same to me. But not you, Harry Moon. I'd never forget you. No, I remember your face. You've gotten in my way before, and I think it's about time for some payback."

67

"Yeah," the snowman to his right said. Harry was pretty sure this was Ug. "I hope you like the Snow, Harry Moon. Because you're about to be buried in it!"

Marcus took another step forward. "I hope you're ready, Harry," he said. "I've been waiting for this for a very long t—"

He was interrupted by a snowball that hit him directly in the chest. As Marcus stumbled backward and dropped his own snowball in surprise, Harry turned around and saw Declan smiling widely.

"Bad guys are stupid," he said. "They spend too much time talking."

"You're going to regret that," Marcus said through his ski mask. "Snowmen, attack!"

Before Harry had time to duck for cover, he was hit in the side of the face with a snowball. It was not very hard, but it was cold and unexpected. He barely had time to feel the sting of it before another snowball hit him in the knee.

Beside him, Hao was tossing a snowball, but he missed his target. As he gathered up another one, three snowballs hit him: one in the chest and two in the back. Harry then realized that the evil snowmen were being very smart about their attack. They were circling them, forming a ring around the Good Mischief Team so they could not escape.

Harry grabbed one of the sleds and chunked it down in the snow in front of him so that it stood up like a little wall in the snow. Right away, it was pelted by snowballs. The brief cover gave him enough time to form his own snowball. He popped up over the cover of the sled and fired it off at Marcus. Marcus ducked, and the snowball hit another of the snowmen in the head. The ski mask was knocked to the side, and Harry saw that it *was* Titus.

No, not Titus, Harry thought. He and the mayor's youngest son had never been best friends by any means, but they had just started to develop a very fragile friendship. Harry knew that Titus was always torn between serving his father and doing the right thing. It made him feel bad for Titus, but not in that moment as he and the rest of the Good Mischief Team were being attacked by snowballs.

"Harry, how are they making so many snowballs?" Declan asked.

Harry ducked down behind the sled for cover again, catching a snowball to the right shoulder as he did so.

"I don't know," Harry said. But he thought he did. In the same way he could sometimes tap into the Good Magic for help, he knew that Mayor Kligore and his family had access to an entirely different kind of magic—something sinister and dark.

To Harry's left, Hao suddenly cried out. He had been struck in the stomach with a large snowball and had fallen down. He was struggling to get up but was pelted by more snowballs from all directions. Harry saw that a cloud of snow was forming behind Marcus and creating snowballs like some weird snowball-making machine. He could see Oink behind that cloud, making snowballs with a speed that hurt Harry's eyes to watch.

As soon as the snowballs were made, Titus and Ug were grabbing them and throwing them. Marcus, meanwhile, was leading them forward, armed with snowballs he was quickly making on his own.

Harry, Bailey, and Declan tried to fight them off, but they were simply outmatched. For every single snowball they could create, the evil snowmen were tossing five or six. Harry didn't know if Oink was using some sort of bad magic or if he was just really skilled at making snowballs.

Hao was still being attacked out there on the ground. The snowmen wouldn't even let him get to his feet. Seeing this, Harry forgot about snowballs for a moment. He shrugged off his backpack and unzipped it. He reached

71

in, going for his wand.

Meanwhile, Declan rolled Hao over onto a sled and pushed off for the hill. Within a second or two, they started riding down the hill together. As they retreated, they called back to Harry and Bailey. "Bailey! Harry! Come on. Get out of there!"

That's when the sled that had been covering Harry seemed to explode. The largest snowball yet struck it dead on, splintering it into little plastic shards. It sent Harry sprawling backward, stumbling in the snow.

He managed to get to his feet just before he went stumbling down Haunted Hill, his backpack half-off of his shoulders. He reached for his wand, but could not seem to get a handle on it.

"Listen to your friends," Marcus said as the evil snowmen surrounded him and Bailey. "Get out of here. Snow day is over."

"And what if we don't?" Bailey asked. He was trying to be brave, but Harry could hear the fear in his voice.

In response, Ug threw a snowball with surprising speed. Harry barely saw it at all before it struck him directly in the face. He stumbled backward again, and his foot landed on something slick. Before he knew it, he had lost his footing and was falling. His feet had been knocked out from under him, and he went down with his feet kicking at the air. When he came back down on the ground, he was sitting on something solid and barreling down Haunted Hill.

13

He looked down and saw that his butt had landed squarely on Declan's baking sheet. He was zipping down the hill sideways on the speedy makeshift sled. A little scared now, Harry tried to get a grip on the sides of the sheet but every bump he hit made it next to impossible. As he tried grabbing on to the sides, he saw that Bailey was behind him, riding down the last remaining plastic sled to get away from the snowmen at the top of the hill.

When Harry turned back around toward the

74

approaching street, he tried to lean forward to better guide the cookie sheet. But he quickly saw that it was too late. He had come to the bottom of the hill and was now only inches away from the curb at the edge of Paul Revere Avenue.

When the baking sheet struck the snowy curb, it was like a race car hitting a ramp. Harry went airborne, higher than Declan had gone earlier. The baking sheet flew out from under him, and for a moment, Harry Moon was flying.

He let out a shout as he started to come down. He did his best to tuck himself into a ball, fearing the pain that was to come when he hit the ground. When he finally *did* land, it was on the other side of the street. He had cleared Paul Revere Avenue and crashed down into the snow on the opposite side of the street.

75

He landed hard, and his right ankle bent in a weird position, twisting in a way the human body should not twist. A flare of pain shot through his body, and he opened his mouth to scream, *before* realizing he had landed face down in the snow.

His three friends were at his side at once, helping him into a sitting position. As Harry knocked the snow from his face, his ankle kept sending bolts of pain through him. He tried moving it, and that only made it hurt worse.

"Are you okay?" Declan asked.

"I don't know," Harry said, trying to get to his feet.

Above them, they could hear the sounds of cackling laughter. They looked up and saw the four evil snowmen. From where Harry and his friends were gathered in the street, the snowmen looked like little white specks on top of Haunted Hill.

"What do we do now?" Hao asked. He was clearly angry from having been so badly beaten, but he also looked a little scared. There was a scratch on his chin, and his bottom lip was bleeding a little from the snowball he had taken directly to the face.

"We regroup," Harry said.

But as he got to his feet, his right leg would not support him. He fell back down into the snow, wondering if he had broken his ankle.

At the top of the hill, the snowmen continued to laugh.

THE THING BEHIND
THE THING

I t took a while, but Harry was finally able to put weight on his foot. The Good Mischief Team had nearly made it back to the Moon house when Harry was able to hobble along on his own. His ankle was still sore, but at least he could use it. Suddenly, though, walking through the snow was more of a chore than a delight.

As they made their way along the streets, they passed several other kids playing in the snow. It was like one big party in town. Harry was beginning to understand that the snow had done much more than just cancel school and keep him from taking his dreaded algebra test. It had made the roads pretty much impossible to drive on (not helped by the inexperienced plow drivers), so a lot of adults had also stayed at home, unable to make it in to work.

Harry saw grown-ups playing with their kids in the snow. Some were making snowmen, others were making snow angels, and others were just running around in it. It warmed Harry's heart to see it, even after the defeat he and the Good Mischief Team had taken at the hands of Marcus Kligore and his band of evil snowmen.

"So, we know that was the Kligore brothers and their cronies, right?" Bailey said as they came to the intersection where they would split up and go to their own homes.

"Yeah," Harry said.

Declan looked at his phone and shook his head. "Harry, it's only noon. They've got the rest of the day to spread terror around town. What can we do?"

Secretly, Harry hoped the call to the police that his mother had placed might do some good. Harry wasn't too sure about how the police worked—especially in a town that was run by Mayor Kligore. Besides, Harry was pretty sure it would take more than a stern talking to in order to get the group of evil snowmen to stop.

"Well," Hao said. "I told Mom I'd be back home for lunch, so I need to get going. She's going to *love* these bumps and bruises I got in the fight," he said sarcastically.

"Okay," Harry said. "Does everyone just want to meet back at my house around one o'clock?"

"Sounds like a plan," Declan said. "I should get home and thaw out, anyway. I haven't been able to feel my nose for a while."

Harry hadn't been able to feel his nose either, but he thought the snowball he had taken to the face had more to do with that than anything else.

"You going to be okay, Harry?" Bailey asked.

"Yeah," he said. "It's just another block. I'll be okay. See you guys in an hour."

With that, the Good Mischief Team went their separate ways. Harry hoped there was more cocoa mix at home. He could sure use some thawing out. He also thought that he should put some ice on his ankle, which was ironic, seeing as how it was so cold outside.

Harry passed another house with two kids and a mom building a snowman out front. They had put a scarf and a carrot nose on it. It looked amazing and pretty charming compared to the monstrous snowmen that had attacked

Harry and his friends on Haunted Hill.

He was so caught up in watching the family build their cool snowman that he almost hobbled right into the man coming down the street in front of him. He looked up and was surprised to see Samson Dupree—owner of the Sleepy Hollow Magic Shoppe and Harry's mentor.

"Harry!" Samson said. "Out enjoying the snow, I see?"

81

"Yeah, I guess so," Harry said.

Samson was dressed in his usual attire. Apparently, the cold temperatures that had come with the snow did not bother him. His purple robe was speckled with flakes, and the crown on his head seemed to shine brighter than ever amid all of the white.

"I see you're sort of limping along there," Samson said. "Sledding accident?"

"You could say that," Harry said. He gave

Samson a quizzical look. He was well aware that Samson sometimes knew things that he couldn't possibly know. He also seemed to show up at the most opportune times even when Harry wasn't thinking of heading to the Magic Shoppe. It all made Harry wonder if Samson knew about the confrontation with the evil snowmen.

"Well, whatever it was," Samson said, "I hope it hasn't ruined this magnificent day." Samson looked up into the sky with a smile on his face. Even though the snow was no longer falling, there was still something beautiful about the white-and-gray sky. It seemed alive and fat with promise—a promise of more snow, perhaps.

"I take it you like the snow?" Harry asked.

"Oh, yes indeed," Samson said. "As a purveyor of magic, I find snow fascinating. There's just something so . . . so . . . well, magical about snow."

"Magical?" Harry asked. "You really think so?"

"Oh, absolutely. The snow is a pure shade of white, and when enough of it falls, it covers up all of the ugliness. Even the creepy stripped trees out in the cemetery are suddenly beautiful. My, oh my, I have missed the snow."

"It is pretty great," Harry agreed.

"Now, this wounded foot of yours," Samson

83

said. "Is it very bad?"

"It's sore. I think I just twisted it pretty bad while sledding."

"Just sledding, huh?" Samson asked with a knowing frown.

"Well, maybe there were others involved. Bullies, you could say."

"Yes, I've heard whispers of some evil-looking snowmen wreaking havoc in town. But they don't bother me too much. Bullies hiding behind masks. There's no real threat there."

"I don't know," Harry said. "They were pretty mean. Strong, too."

"Ah, but you're still up and walking so they can't be but so strong," Samson said with a reassuring laugh. "Remember, Harry, bullies are always looking for something. And most of the time, it's the thing behind the thing that they are looking for."

"The thing behind the thing?" Harry asked. "What's that mean?"

"Well, bullies are rarely mean for the sake of just being mean. Something drives them."

"I'm not sure I follow you," Harry said.

"Yes, the mind of a bully can be quite confusing," Samson said. "I know they may seem scary, but they are really no different than you or me. Just like us, bullies are seeking something, Harry."

Harry liked Samson a great deal, but when the man started to speak in riddles like this, it made Harry frustrated and a little uncomfortable. He could only nod at what Samson said as his mentor wiped stray snowflakes from his purple robe.

"Anyway, be well, Harry. I trust you'll enjoy the rest of this fantastic snow day!"

"I'll try," Harry said.

He watched Samson go, his purple robe almost impossibly bright against the world of white that Sleepy Hollow had become.

The thing behind the thing, Harry thought. *What on earth is that supposed to mean?*

With that thought tucked safely in his head, he limped on toward home. For the first time all day, the snow started to feel like a burden, like something he had to endure. Rather than be excited about the rest of the day, he now saw it as cold and tough to walk through. Now, he saw it as a symbol of the defeat he and the Good Mischief Team had suffered at the hands of the evil snowmen.

And an angry part of him sort of wished it would all just melt away.

THE FOUR SNOWMEN OF THE SNOWPOCALYPSE

He felt ridiculous doing it, but the first thing Harry did when he entered the house was to put ice on his busted ankle. He sat down in one of the kitchen chairs, propped his foot up in another, and placed an icepack on it. After a few moments, Honey came into the kitchen, once again bundled up to head back outside.

"Oh my goodness," she yelled when she saw his ankle. It was slightly swollen, and a purple bruise had formed there. "What happened?"

"The snowmen," Harry said.

"I told you not to go after them," Honey said.

88

"I know. But someone has to try something. These guys are out of hand."

Honey went to the kitchen counter and started making a mug of cocoa for Harry. She kept looking back at him, as if she was very concerned for him.

"You're all bundled up again," Harry pointed out. "Are you going back out?"

"Yeah. We're going to sled in Claire's yard. Her mom is there and is going to watch us. So, if the snowmen show up again, there will be an adult. Just in case."

"That's a good idea. Hey, speaking of adults, where are Mom and Dad?"

"Dad went down to the town garage to see if he could do anything to help with plowing the roads. Mom took Harvest over to Ladybug Trail where there's supposed to be a little hill where all the smaller kids are sledding."

Harry nodded, glad that his mom wasn't home to go nuts over the condition of his ankle. Harry couldn't help but grimace when he looked at it so he knew his mother would be worried out of her mind.

89

Honey brought the mug of steaming cocoa to him and placed it on the table in front of him.

"Thanks," he said, immediately lifting the cocoa to his mouth and taking a sip.

"Well, I'm out of here for now," Honey said.

"Okay. Be careful."

"I will." And with that, Honey did something Harry did not expect. She walked over to him and kissed him on the cheek. "Thanks for going after those bullies for me," she said.

Before Harry had time to say you're welcome, Honey was out of the back door and headed out to her next little adventure.

Harry remained in his chair with his leg propped up until the ice pack was just too much to handle. He removed it and then hobbled over to the fridge where he made a sandwich for lunch. As he ate it, he thought about the horrible fight between the Good Mischief Team and the evil snowmen.

The Four Snowmen of the Snowpocalypse, Harry thought with a nervous grin. They were certainly spooky, and it seemed they would stop at nothing to prevent the kids of Sleepy Hollow from having fun in the snow. But why?

Harry just knew that Mayor Kligore had to be at the center of it. He also had a sneaking suspicion that the mayor had somehow prevented snow from visiting the town for all these years, until now. Harry wondered if some sort of mistake had been made, and now, the mayor was doing whatever he could to inflict as much misery as he could.

It was just a guess, really, but Harry was pretty sure he was right.

As he was finishing up his sandwich, someone knocked on the back door. When Harry saw that it was Bailey he waved him in, not yet ready to stand back up on his wounded ankle. The small trip from the table to the fridge had been pretty bad.

Bailey knocked snow from his boots before coming inside. He took a seat next to Harry and let out a sigh.

"Something wrong?" Harry asked.

Instead of answering Harry, Bailey reached into his coat pocket and took out his phone. He opened up his Twitter app and scrolled around for a bit. He pulled up someone's profile and handed it over to Harry.

The profile's username was KLIGDOG. It was a name that Harry knew right away. It was, after all, pretty famous around Sleepy Hollow Middle and High School. It was Marcus Kligore's Twitter handle.

Harry scrolled through the last few updates. What he saw stirred anger like hornets inside of him. There was picture after picture of kids that the evil snowmen had bullied. Some were covered in snow while others were running away in tears. One picture showed Marcus in his scary snowman outfit breaking a wooden sled over his knee. Behind him, a young boy sat on the ground in tears as the other snowmen crowded around him.

The caption under this picture read, This is how you REALLY enjoy a snow day!!!

One of the last pictures Harry saw showed his own screaming face as he sped awkwardly down Haunted Hill on the baking sheet. There was no caption for this picture, just a hashtag:

#MoonMan

Disgusted, Harry slid the phone back to Bailey.

"We have to do something don't we Harry?" Bailey asked.

Harry nodded. He felt that they did need to do something. But the ache in his ankle was a clear reminder of what had happened the last time they had come face-to-face with what he thought of as the Four Snowmen of the Snowpocalypse.

"Any ideas?" Bailey asked.

Harry hated to admit it, but the idea of facing the snowmen again scared him. He was not yet ready to try sledding again in an attempt to lure the snowmen out. And even if he was, he was pretty sure his ankle was not ready to climb any hills.

"Maybe we could just go out and do something easy," Harry suggested. "Something

93

little, like building a snowman. Maybe that would bring them out."

"I don't know," Bailey said. "We built that awesome fort this morning, and they never showed up."

"My parents where home then," Harry pointed out. "Maybe that kept them away."

94

Bailey nodded as another knock sounded at the door. Hao came in and took his own seat at the table. Declan came in only seconds behind him. "So, what are we doing now?" he asked.

"I think we're building a snowman," Harry said.

The other three boys gave a shrug all at the same time. It wasn't nearly as exciting as sledding down Haunted Hill, but they'd still be out playing in the snow. They filed out of the house and went into the Moon's front yard. So far, the only disturbance in the snow out front were a few trails of footprints. Harry could see tiny ones where Harvest had apparently tried to walk in the snow before being picked up by their mother.

Together, the Good Mischief Team started to create a huge snowball for the base of the snowman. Having never made one before, they felt the need to make their first creation a truly spectacular specimen. They wanted it to be huge, to tower over anyone that might pass by in the streets—especially the Four Snowmen of the Snowpocalypse.

When they reached the point where Harry needed to go into the garage for the step ladder to put the middle section on the lower part of the body, they noticed a group of kids running down the street. The kids were coming in their direction, running hard through the snow. Some of them fell down a few times only to get back up and keep speeding ahead. Harry counted five of them in all. From what he could see, they looked to be no older than nine or so.

The boy in the lead looked familiar. Harry thought it might be one of Honey's friends from school, but he wasn't sure. All Harry knew for certain was that the kid was crying and looked scared out of his mind.

As the group staggered by Harry and his friends, the lead kid stumbled in the snow. Declan was there right away to help him to his feet. "Hey, hey, slow down," Declan said. "What's the matter?" The kid wiped snot away from his nose with a snow-covered mitten and drew in a shaky breath. It was clear that he was trying not to cry in front of older kids.

"We were sledding and throwing snowballs over at the pumpkin p-p-patch," the kid said, struggling to get the words out. "And these four monsters showed up—these snowmen with big claws and scary f-f-faces!"

"Did they hurt you?" Harry asked.

97

"Just some hard snowballs," another of the kids said. He looked embarrassed and clearly ready to be out of the cold.

"But they broke my sled," another of the kids said, also near tears.

"Yeah, and knocked over the igloo we had spent hours making," said another of the kids. This was a girl, and it was clear that she had also been crying.

"Well," Harry said, unsure of anything else to say. "Just be careful on your way home, okay?

Maybe stay inside for a while."

The lead kid nodded, and the others followed him when he started walking farther down the street. Harry and the Good Mischief Team watched them go, their massive snowman forgotten for the moment.

The four of them looked at one another. Their fear and frustration was easy to see on their faces. Then, for the second time that day, a decision was made without any of them having to speak a word.

"Should we go sledding again?" Declan asked.

"Yeah, is your ankle up to it?" Hao asked.

"I don't know," Harry said. "But you know what? I have a better idea. We need to be ready this time. We need to have the upper hand."

"How?"

Harry thought about it for a moment, and

a small smile crept onto his face. "You guys run back home and get as many buckets as you can find. Then meet me at the town square in an hour, right under the Headless Horseman statue."

"What for?" Bailey asked.

"Do you guys trust me?" Harry asked.

"Absolutely," Declan said. Hao and Bailey nodded in agreement.

99

"Good," Harry said. "Just keep an eye on your phones, and meet me there in one hour. Can you do that?"

His three friends nodded and headed off in their separate directions. They left Harry alone in the yard with the snowman that, Harry assumed, would likely never be finished.

Before heading inside, Harry gave the snowman a loving little pat on its backside. He then limped back inside with an idea forming in his head.

100

#MoonMansChallenge

Inside, Harry Moon set a tea kettle on the stove and set about making the fourth batch of hot chocolate for the day. As he waited for the water to boil and the kettle to whistle, he pulled out his phone and plopped down at the table. He opened his Twitter account—which he rarely used because of his parents' views on social media—and started to type.

He read it over before posting it to his meager thirty-one followers. When he was satisfied with the message, it read, Bullies are cowards. Are they as scary when we KNOW they're coming? Let's find out under the Headless Horseman. See you there at 4:00, @ KLIGDOG.

When he posted the message, his heart seemed to shudder. The fear he'd felt from earlier in the morning was coming back. It seemed to radiate from his injured ankle this time. Doing his best to ignore it, Harry went to his piled winter clothes by the back door and started to bundle up again.

As he was putting on his boots, a familiar hopping noise met his ears. When he looked up, he saw Rabbit sitting at the kitchen table. He was looking at Harry's phone, frowning at the message Harry had just tweeted.

"Do you think this was the best idea?" Rabbit asked.

"I don't know," Harry said. "But I feel like I have to do something!"

"Why?" Rabbit asked. "Since when were you elected to be the hero of Sleepy Hollow?"

"I wasn't. But bullying is wrong."

Rabbit nodded, sliding the phone away. "It is indeed," he said. "But what you plan on doing is more like revenge than justice. There's a saying about revenge. Something about eating it as a dish best served cold, I think."

103

"What?" Harry asked.

"It comes from the French sometime in the 1800s, so take it with a grain of salt. Anyway, that's not the point. I fear you're confusing 'doing the right thing' with 'vengeance.' And the Great Magician is quite clear on his feelings on vengeance. Repaying evil for evil is not going to get anything done, Harry."

"I suppose you're going to throw in something about being kind to your enemies now, huh?"

"You said it, not me," Rabbit said.

The kettle whistled on the stove. Harry went to it and started filling thermoses for the Good Mischief Team. When he was done, he had just enough to make a small cup for his usually invisible friend. He handed it to Rabbit and watched as he sniffed at it and carefully picked up the warm mug.

"I don't want to *hurt* anyone," Harry said. "I just want to show them and the other kids in town that it doesn't pay to be a bully."

"Ah, but is it your place to give such a lesson?"

"I guess not," Harry said.

Rabbit took a sip of the hot cocoa, and his ears perked up in straight lines. His eyes grew wide, and he took another huge sip. When

he brought the mug down, there was a wet chocolate moustache on his upper lip.

"Do all things in love, Harry. That is the most important skill of any magician, whether Great or still learning. Just remember that when you set out on this mission you have set up for yourself."

"I spoke with Samson earlier," Harry said. "He said bullies aren't being mean just to be mean. He says there's something behind it all."

"Ah yes, the thing behind the thing," Rabbit said as if it made perfect sense.

"What does that mean?" Harry asked.

"Well, look at it from your eyes," Rabbit said. "Why do you care so much about standing up for the kids that have been bullied today?"

106

"Because what Marcus, Titus, Oink, and Ug are doing is wrong. And someone needs to stop them."

"So, your need to stand up for the little kids is driving you to confront Marcus and his pals. You are not being violent or confrontational just to start a fight. You are doing it for some sort of justice, and *that* is your thing behind the thing. So now, what do you think it is for Marcus and Titus?"

Harry knew the answer right away, and it

all started to make sense. "Mayor Kligore," he said. "They just want to make their dad proud of them."

Rabbit nodded, but all Harry could see was his ears. His face was blocked by the mug that he was once again gulping from.

"Keep that in mind when you're out there, Harry," Rabbit said, wiping hot chocolate away from the fur around his mouth. "And if you should lose again, don't be discouraged. If you handle this the right way, even your defeat can be an example to those young kids you're trying to stand up for."

"You think we'll be defeated?" Harry asked.

His cup now empty, Rabbit hopped down from the table and looked up at Harry. "I think there is a chance, yes. But winning or losing is not the important thing here. The important thing is to do all things in love."

Harry nodded, understanding perfectly. Still, he was unable to stop the snarky thought that

107

passed through his head.

Yeah? Tell that to my ankle.

The evil snowmen—who had no idea that Harry Moon had started to think of them as the Four Snowmen of the Snowpocalypse but would probably love the title—were gathered together around a large stone fireplace. The fireplace was on the lower level of the Kligore Mansion on Folly Farm. By the crackling flames, they warmed their bones and dried their snowmen costumes.

Behind them, sitting in a large throne-like chair, Mayor Kligore was scrolling through Marcus's Twitter feed. Every now and then he would chuckle or laugh at the carnage he saw. "This is quite good work," he said. "I must say, the four of you make a surprisingly good team."

"Thanks, boss," Oink said, far too eager to please.

108

"Ah, oh my!" the mayor said with a sinister grin. "I see you even got the best of Harry Moon! Look at the face on him!"

"Yeah, he was easy," Marcus said, warming his hands by the fire. "The little goon went rolling down that hill, screaming the whole way."

"Yeah, he was easy," Titus said.

Titus was unable to look at his father, though. Honestly, he *had* enjoyed himself today. A lot of what they had done was mean and very unnecessary, but the snow had made it all fun. And the look on his father's face; well, Titus could not remember the last time he had seen his dad so happy.

109

As the mayor continued to scroll, his eyes suddenly narrowed, and he looked very confused. That confusion then turned to anger, causing him to leap up out of his chair.

"Marcus, have you seen this?" he asked.

"Seen what?"

"This tweet from Harry Moon. He tagged you in it."

"Let me see that," Marcus said, snatching the phone from his father's hand. He read what was on the screen and then looked to his three partners in crime. The look of anger that spread across his face was identical to that of his father's.

"Oh, I don't believe this!" he shouted.

"What?" Titus asked.

"That little creep is calling me out! Harry Moon has tagged me and challenged all of us!"

He handed the phone to Titus, who also read Harry's tweet. The phone was passed around to all of the fake snowmen and then, finally, back to Mayor Kligore.

"What do you think we should do, Dad?" Marcus asked.

"Simple," Mayor Kligore said with a crooked

smile. "You suit back up and continue to terrorize the town. And when four o'clock rolls around, you be there to meet him. And I want you to make an example out of him and his little friends. I want you to hurt him if you have to. Nothing that will get you in trouble, of course. But enough to make him think twice about every crossing us again!"

Positively fuming, Marcus nodded and snatched up his white hoodie and ski mask. He looked at the sneering smile on the mask and smiled right back at it.

111

Titus watched his older brother and cringed. There was an anger in Marcus that sometimes scared Titus. Under the ladies' man charm and careless spoiled teenager façade, there was something positively dark and evil. In that moment, Titus wasn't sure about heading back out. He didn't want anyone to get hurt. Sure, some teasing and name-calling here and there was one thing but hurting people on purpose was totally different.

Still, it was rare that his father was ever this

happy, and he was *never* this proud of his sons. Titus watched as Marcus started to get dressed again, slipping the white pants and hoodie on. Beside him, Oink and Ug did the same. With a heavy heart, Titus pulled the snowman costume on once again.

He was glad when the ski mask covered his face. That way, his father would only see the evil grin on the mask and not the trembling frown on his face.

THE GREAT SNOW WAR ON THE TOWN SQUARE

The Good Mischief Team gathered under the statue of the Headless Horseman at 3:15 that afternoon. Hao was the last to arrive. He had run into yet another group of youngsters that had been terrorized by the bully snowmen and had taken some time to calm them down. When he got to the town square, he was holding his phone out and peering down at it. In his other hand, he held a large bucket that he'd found in his garage.

"Harry," Hao said. "Um, are you sure about this? This tweet . . . it could cause a lot of trouble."

"No way," Bailey said. "I think it was awesome. It was a great way to call out Marcus. Let him sit on *that* for a little while!"

"Still," Hao said, "this could get bad. We already got humiliated by them once."

"Yes, but we'll be ready this time," Harry said.

Behind him, tucked away at the sides of the Headless Horseman statue, were the five buckets they had acquired so far. Adding Hao's to the pile would give them six. One of the buckets was already nearly filled with nice, round, fully packed snowballs. The four of them went to work and started making more. Within five minutes, two more buckets were filled to the brim.

Bailey stopped to take a break, and when he did, he used his phone to check in on Harry's tweet. "Whoa," he said. "Um . . . Harry?"

"Yeah?"

"This tweet of yours is getting around. It's been re-tweeted fifteen times, and it's got thirty-seven likes."

"But I don't even have that many followers!" Harry exclaimed.

"I guess it's making the rounds," Bailey said. "There are people commenting on it too. Here's one that says 'Go get 'em Harry!' And another one says 'Bullies stink!' Oh, and here's one from Sarah Sinclair. It says 'Be careful out there, Harry!' And then there's a kissy face."

Harry blushed and was slightly embarrassed. He wasn't sure how to feel, knowing that his tweet was getting so much attention. He knew one thing for sure, though. If his tweet was becoming popular so quickly (well, popular for Sleepy Hollow's standards, anyway), then Marcus Kligore had surely seen it by now.

Harry looked around, making sure Marcus and his other fake snowmen hadn't decided to show up early. So far, there was no sign of them. But Harry *did see* that a few kids had come to the edges of the snow-covered lawn of the town square. He hadn't thought about that. By sending out such a public challenge to Marcus on Twitter, others had seen it and wanted to catch a glimpse of the aftermath.

In other words, if the Four Snowmen of the Snowpocalypse defeated them again, this time a lot of kids might see it.

Suddenly, Harry was starting to think that this was not such a great idea after all. But it was too late now. It was 3:52, and they had six buckets packed with snowballs. They also had their two remaining sleds and Declan's baking tray.

116

Harry was also aware of his backpack. He felt its light weight on his back and knew that if he needed it, his wand was there. He hoped it wouldn't come to that. He hated to use the Good Magic for things like this, especially after his talks with Samson and Rabbit earlier in the day. Besides, if he was doing this to stand up for the kids that were being bullied, he'd rather not use magic. The other kids didn't have access to the Good Magic like he did, so he felt that using it might be slightly unfair.

117

Harry checked the Clock Tower at the outer edge of the town square and saw it ticking closer to 4:00. There was no backing down now. There was no way to gracefully bow out after making such a public challenge.

"They're here!"

Someone from the small yet still-gathering crowd at the edge of the town square was pointing behind the Good Mischief Team, farther out in the snow. Harry turned in that direction and saw the four white figures walking across Main Street, heading straight for them.

Marcus and his fellow evil snowmen were just as terrifying as Harry remembered. Even though Harry was well aware that they were wearing ski masks, the beast-like faces looked real. The same could be said for the rubber gloves they wore on their hands. Those black claws looked deadly as the snowmen drew closer.

"Get ready, guys," Harry said. He slowly backed closer toward the statue where the six buckets of snowballs were hidden. Bailey, Declan, and Hao all did the same.

Harry took a good look around. The Four Snowmen of the Snowpocalypse were nearly there now. The crowd of spectators had grown to nearly twenty kids. They were standing in a scattered circle around the Headless Horsemen, giving the Good Mischief Team and the evil snowmen a large arena of snow to do battle in.

The four snowmen stepped into the town square and came forward. As they passed the ring of kids, Marcus pushed a small boy to the ground. "Out of my way," he said. He then directed his attention to Harry and chuckled.

"You've got to be stupid to call me out like this," Marcus said.

A thousand replies came to Harry, but he kept them all to himself. He was still trying to stay on the right side of the line that sat between standing up for what was right and carrying out the kind of justice that was not his to hand out.

He took a step backward, closer to their hidden snowball stash. As he backed up, his ankle reminded him that it was not in the best shape.

"Well, you asked for it, Moon Man," Marcus said. "Oink, if you please."

With that, Oink stepped forward. He was wearing a strange-looking back pack that he shrugged from his shoulders. He set it on the ground at his feet with a dirty little chuckle. He kicked it open, and Harry saw softball-sized snowballs spill out. Some of them were made of solid chunks of ice.

"Harry?" Bailey said from beside him, clearly alarmed by the sight of the ice.

Harry felt his concern too. Getting pegged by a snowball was one thing. But if you got hit hard enough with a solid chunk of ice, it could do some real damage. Bones could be broken. Teeth could be knocked out.

But Harry didn't have time to think twice. Even if he had wanted to retreat, there was no time, for that was when Ug acted quickly and threw the first snowball.

After that, everything happened far too quickly as the town square became a snowy battle field of epic proportions.

The first snowball hit Declan in the shoulder but did no real damage. In response, Declan only stepped back, luring the evil snowmen into their trap. Marcus threw the next snowball and then Titus. Both hit Harry, once in the leg and once in the arm. Harry backed away, acting scared (which wasn't hard to do) and uncertain.

121

But when the snowmen had come forward several more steps, the Good Mischief Team sprang into action. They each reached into one of the buckets they had filled and grabbed several snowballs. They started throwing them right away, taking the evil snowmen completely by surprise.

The first one Harry threw hit Oink directly in the face. Beside him, Declan tossed one in a speedy overhanded throw that struck Titus in the stomach. Both of them stumbled backward and fell to the ground. Hao was next, throwing one at Marcus that bounced harmlessly off of his knee. Harry followed up next, throwing two snowballs at the same time.

One missed Marcus completely, but the other one hit him in the chest. As Marcus drew back to throw one at Harry, Declan threw another one that caught Marcus on his elbow. As he dropped his snowball, Marcus was hit with another . . . and then another.

122

It was hard for Harry to see much of anything as he threw snowball after snowball. The square had become nothing more than a white blur to him as snowballs whizzed past his face. The one thing Harry *could* see was that it appeared they were winning. He and the Good Mischief Team were tossing snowballs as quickly as they could. Two buckets were already empty, and they started to work on the third.

Oink and Ug were on the ground, crawling away and catching snowballs to their backside. Titus was backing away but still throwing the occasional snowball that either went wide or landed just at the feet of the person it was aimed at. Meanwhile, Marcus did his best to stand his ground. He was still pelting snowballs as he was nailed time and time again. He was roaring with anger as he took snowballs to the head, chest, and legs.

When he was hit in the hip by a large snowball tossed by Declan, Marcus stumbled back and fell on his butt. A plume of snow drifted up as he hit the ground. All around the circle of kids watching the battle, children started to snicker and laugh. The town square went silent for a moment as Marcus got to his feet. With a look of absolute rage on his face, he reached down to the backpack Oink had brought with them.

He grabbed one of the iceballs and threw it hard, like he was throwing a fastball at a baseball game. Harry leaped out of the way at the last second. When he hit the ground, he looked back just in time to see the iceball clip Declan's elbow. Declan yelled out in pain, dropping the snowball he was holding and going to his knees.

Oink joined Marcus, throwing an iceball of his own. This one came at Harry, and if he had not thought quickly, yanking one of the sleds up in front of his head, the iceball would have smashed him right between the eyes. Instead, it crashed against the sled, sending a crack down the center of it.

With the cracked sled held out like a shield, Harry ran to Declan and helped him behind the cover of the Headless Horseman statue. Iceballs and snowballs struck the sled and pinged off the statue as they ducked down for cover.

"Are you okay?" Harry asked.

"I think so," Declan said, hissing in pain.

"Stay here and—"

An iceball smashed into the statue just over his head. The sound it made was like a bell, if a bell could get angry.

Harry peered out and saw that Hao and

Bailey were alone against all four of the snowmen. "Just stay here," Harry said.

He went back out with the sled as a shield again. He dashed over to the three remaining buckets of snowballs. He gathered up some ammo and started throwing. Marcus dodged the first two but the third hit Titus in the shoulder. Titus returned fire, striking Harry in the leg before Harry could block the shot with his shield.

125

Harry aimed for Marcus again, his busted ankle now screaming in pain. His snowball fell short, and Marcus wasted no time in firing back. He faked a throw at Harry and then delivered a screeching iceball at Bailey.

Harry saw it happen as if it was in slow motion. The iceball smashed into the right side of Bailey's face, just above his mouth. Bailey dropped to the ground right away, covering his head and hollering in pain. He scrambled for the cover of the Headless Horseman statue and hunkered down there.

Before he was completely hidden, Harry saw the shape his friend was in. His cheek was already swelling and his upper lip had been busted open. He could see red drops of Bailey's blood speckling the snow.

This is getting out of hand, Harry thought. *I have to stop it somehow. I'm going to have to use magic.*

He was distracted just long enough for Marcus to throw a speeding iceball at him. Harry did not see it in time, and it slammed into his stomach. In an instant, all of the wind was knocked out of him. He doubled over, doing everything he could to not fall over. Meanwhile, poor Hao was battling Oink and Ug on his own. He was losing badly as he was backed into the statue and getting nailed over and over with snowballs.

Marcus came over and leered down at Harry from behind the snowman ski mask. He tossed a plain snowball hard at Harry's right leg, knocking him down to his knees. He then held a huge iceball in his right hand and held it over

his head, preparing to throw it down hard onto Harry.

"You'll think twice before trying to call me out and embarrass me again, won't you?" Marcus said. "I know you think you're special, but you're just a weak little brat like every other sniveling snot in this town."

Harry knew he could do nothing. He had no time to go for his wand. And even if he tried to dodge the iceball, it was only going to cause it to hit somewhere else, hurting him and slowing him down.

127

This is going to hurt, Harry thought.

But then, out of the corner of his eye, Harry spotted something behind Marcus.

One of the snowmen—Titus, if Harry was guessing right—was picking up a snowball as discreetly as he could. He lobbed it underhanded very fast, making sure no one else saw what he was doing.

The snowball arched through the air, not fast at all, and smacked Marcus directly on the back of his head.

"What the—" Marcus said.

But he was interrupted by another snowball. This one hit him so perfectly in the mouth that it stuck there. For a moment, it looked like he was eating a snow cone without the cone.

Harry looked around for who had thrown the snowball. It was a girl, standing just in front of the ring of spectators. It was a girl he knew well—a girl he loved dearly.

"Honey?" he asked.

"That's right," she said, packing another snowball. "If you're going to fight dirty, so are we!"

"We?" Marcus asked, stalking toward her and spitting snow out of mouth. "Are you telling me that you want to get the same beating your brother and his loser friends are getting?"

"No," another kid said from the small crowd. "She means *we* as in all of us!"

It was then that Harry saw that over half of the kids that had been watching the battle had snowballs in their hands. Their arms were pulled back, ready to throw.

Marcus looked around the crowd, letting out a nervous laugh. "Fine," he said. "If that's the way you want it."

He hefted the iceball back in his hand. Harry acted quickly, throwing a handful of powder into Marcus's face. The moment he spent blinking it away was enough time for the crowd to get their first snowballs sailing through the air.

Most of them struck Marcus, making pleasant popping sounds as they struck him. He threw an arm up to block them off, but it did no good. Oink and Ug took his side, and for a moment, they tried to throw snowballs and iceballs back at the crowd.

It took less than a minute for the Four

Snowmen of the Snowpocalypse to realize that they had lost. What had started out as a four-on-four battle was now more like a thirty-on-four beating. And even though they were armed with powerful iceballs, they were not getting the chance to throw them as they were mauled by snowballs.

Eventually, Marcus dashed out of the square and back across Main Street. The other three snowmen followed him. As they made their way across the street in retreat, Harry locked eyes with Titus. If not for Titus, Harry was pretty sure his face would be all busted up right now. Titus had saved him—and had made sure no one had seen him do it.

When the four evil snowmen were across the street and running farther off into the distance, the kids in the town square cheered. The sound warmed Harry's heart as he went behind the Headless Horseman statue to check on his friends.

Declan's elbow was bruised and swollen pretty badly. But it wasn't nearly as bad as Bailey's

busted lip and swollen cheek. As for Hao, he had come out of it all with just a few scratches on his arms and forehead.

"How about that?" Hao asked, looking around at the crowd of kids.

Harry looked at Honey, who was high-fiving the girl in the crowd next to her. Although he seemed to hurt everywhere, Harry couldn't help but smile. His ankle was still very sore, and the blast he'd taken to the stomach was making it hard to breathe. But all of that was easy to ignore in the chorus of cheers from the kids in the town square.

131

132

NIGHT SLEDDING

Just as the sun was setting over Sleepy Hollow, the four evil snowmen that had wreaked so much havoc throughout the town for most of the day approached Mayor Maximus Kligore's house. They left footprints in the snow behind them; a trail that had started at the town square and wound all the way around town to the sidewalk of Kligore Mansion.

They walked very slowly and with their heads hung low. The confident strut they had carried with them through the snow all day was gone. Now, they approached the front door like kids that knew they were in trouble and were about to be scolded.

Even before Marcus was able to knock on the door, it flew open in front of them. Mayor Kligore stood on the other side with a hardened look on his face.

"Get inside," Mayor Kligore barked at them.

They filed into the house quiet and scared. When the door closed behind them, they all jumped in surprise at the same time. Slowly, they all removed their white hoods and the ski masks. Without those two pieces of their outfits on, the rest of the costume looked rather silly. They could have been dressed as fluffy white bunnies rather than malicious snowmen.

"It's all over Twitter," Mayor Kligore said, showing them his phone. "Not only were you defeated, but you were downright *embarrassed!*"

There were pictures of the epic snowball battle, most of them showing how the crowd of kids had stepped in near the last part to send the evil snowmen packing. Marcus looked at the pictures with a hateful sneer.

"They fought dirty," Marcus whined. "When all of those other kids stepped in, we were outnumbered!"

"Well, if you had scared them badly enough the first time, maybe they would have been at home cowering in their rooms rather than out on the streets to watch a snowball fight!" Mayor Kligore yelled.

135

"It was all Harry Moon's fault!" Oink squealed. "He tried to stand up for all the kids, and they came out to cheer him on!"

Mayor Kligore stomped his foot like a spoiled child. "Harry Moon! Will there ever be a time when he doesn't interfere with my plans?"

"I can stop him next time," Marcus said defiantly.

Beside him, Titus let out a quick burst of laughter, which he did his best to bite back. All eyes turned to him, causing him to take a step backward.

"Something funny, son?" Mayor Kligore asked.

"No, sir. I just know that whenever Marcus goes up against Harry it never ends well."

"You little snot!" Marcus said.

"No, no. He's right," Mayor Kligore said. "Maybe next time I'll place something of such importance in the hands of my *other* son."

Marcus shot Titus a look filled with anger. Titus did his best to return it but there was something about his older brother that he had never really trusted. Once again, Titus sensed that looming darkness in his brother. Something impossibly mean was lurking beneath the surface—something dark that Titus had no intention of waking up.

Still quite angry, Mayor Kligore snatched up the ski masks from his four failed snowmen and carried them over to the fireplace.

"I hope you all had fun while it lasted," Mayor Kligore said. "In the end, it was yet another miserable failure at the hands of that wretched little Harry Moon and his friends. What sort of magic did he use this time?"

"Erm, um . . . " Ug said.

"See, the thing is," said Oink.

"He didn't use any," Titus said. "No magic. Just . . . snowballs. And hope."

"Hope?" Mayor Kligore said, spitting the word from his mouth like it was a rotten piece of food.

"The kids that pitched in look up to him," Titus said. "He gives them hope."

"I see," Mayor Kligore said. He carried the ski masks over to the fire and tossed them into the flames. The masks went up quickly, the fabric burning and sending up plumes of gray smoke into the chimney.

"Well then," Mayor Kligore continued, "let's just make sure we work harder in the future to see what we can do to take that hope away."

While the ski masks formerly belonging to the Four Snowmen of the Snowpocalypse went up in flames, several children began to gather together at the top of a small hill on Nightingale Lane. A dozen kids were going up and down the small hill on sleds while other children simply rolled down it. Some elected to slide down on their jacket-covered bellies like penguins.

Harry and Honey Moon were among these kids. Harry enjoyed it, though he took great care to keep his busted ankle from taking on too much activity. His entire family was on the side of the street, watching the kids have fun. He even got to see his father, John Moon, go

138

down the little hill with Harvest in his lap.

The moon was out and someone had started a tiny little bonfire at the edge of the curb at the bottom of the hill. Farther out, Nightingale Lane intersected with Main Street, but there was no traffic. The only vehicle on the road was the rather reckless snowplow as it made its last course of the night. As Harry watched, it accidentally rolled up onto the sidewalk, the plow clanging loudly against the curb.

139

It was an odd feeling, but Harry was pretty sure that everyone in attendance at this small sledding session knew that this would be their last chance to have fun in the snow. He watched the younger kids enjoying the tiny hill and tried to remember what it had been like to blast down Haunted Hill. For some reason that escaped him; it felt like it had happened about a hundred years ago.

Harry rode down to the bottom of the hill, pulling Honey's sled behind him. It was good to hear her laughing after having seen her cry earlier in the day. When they reached the bottom of the hill, Honey headed back up right away. Harry, meanwhile, looked out toward Main Street. The street lamps were reflecting in the snow in a way that was sort of creepy and pretty, all at the same time. The snow itself seemed to have some light to it that was more powerful than the moon.

As he turned to head back up the hill, he saw his mother coming down the hill. She was slowly guiding a sled, taking her turn to give Harvest a ride down. Harvest was clapping his hands and cheering as the sled came to a stop.

Mary Moon looked up at her son with a sneaky sort of grin. "I notice that you've been hobbling around," she said. "You hurt your leg?"

"My ankle," Harry said. "Just a little sledding mishap."

Mary Moon gave him the sort of knowing look that mothers are very good at giving. It told Harry that she knew he might not be telling her the whole truth. "You know," she said, "I heard about an epic snowball fight out at the

town square today. You didn't have anything to do with that, did you?"

"I might have," Harry said, kicking at the snow guiltily with his good foot.

"And would that be how you hurt your ankle?"

"No, that was something different."

"Did it involve sticking up for your sister or any of the other kids that got bullied today?" Mary asked.

141

He smiled, a little embarrassed. "Maybe."

Mary considered this for a moment and then ruffled Harry's hair. When she gave him a quick kiss on his forehead in front of everyone, he didn't even mind. "You know, if I don't tell you enough already, you're a pretty special kid, Harry Moon. But still, please be careful out there."

"Thanks, Mom. And I will."

She smiled at him, and they walked back up the hill together. Harry pulled the sled up, Harvest clinging to it and getting a free ride behind them. Climbing the hill caused Harry's ankle to ache, but he, once again, looked at the smiles and laughter all around him in the midst of the snow.

It all seemed to make the pain fade away.

142

MELTING

Mayor Kligore had hired a professional house cleaner to come into his house during Sleepy Hollow's totally unexpected snow day. He'd paid extra to make sure that any and all traces of the stray cat that Oink had brought in the previous night were eliminated. When he stepped into his office later that night, his office smelled cleaner than it ever had before.

He sat down behind his large desk and pulled out his book of enchantments. He started to go through each and every one just like he did every night before he went to bed. Tonight, he wasted no time going directly to the anti-snow enchantment.

144

In order to carry out these enchantments, he had to call upon forces he made certain deals with long ago. These were the same forces that had granted him the power to control Sleepy Hollow—the same forces that gave him certain dark gifts. He knew that calling out to those forces was dangerous, but he also knew that those forces needed him. That's why he had no fear when he cast his eyes to his book of enchantments and called out for help from an unseen world beyond this one.

He also knew that there were other forces. He believed that these other forces were also at work within Sleepy Hollow, namely in his thirteen-year-old nemesis, Harry Moon. There was always an invisible battle of sorts at play in Sleepy Hollow, and sometimes, they could sneak into the real world—even in the form of something as silly as a snowball fight on the town square.

Sometimes, when Mayor Kligore called upon the dark forces for help, he could sense those other forces trying to stop him. He *did* fear those forces. He knew that they worked to keep things right in town and to bring justice at some point in the future.

With the anti-snow enchantment done, Mayor Kligore looked out his window to his snowcapped yard.

A small black cat marched its way through the snow. A trail of tiny footprints snaked behind it. The cat paused for a moment and seemed to look up at him. He knew it was not possible, but he could have sworn the stupid cat was smiling at him.

Mayor Kligore frowned and closed his blinds. He had other enchantments to do, and if he was lucky, the miserable snow outside would have already started to melt by the time he was done.

Harry Moon jerked awake with a gasp. He looked around his room, sure that something would be there in the darkness ready to eat him. But his room was the same as it always was. Curious and with a slight sense of doom pushing him off the bed, Harry slowly walked to his bedroom window. As he crossed the floor, he looked at his bedside clock, which read 11:33.

Harry looked out of his window and smiled at the snow. Part of him had almost expected it to be gone.

"You okay?" Rabbit asked him from the darkness of his room.

"Yes. I just woke up scared."

"Bad dream?" Rabbit asked.

"No. I felt like . . . I don't know. I felt like I was in danger. I don't know for certain, but I think I can feel the Bad Magic at work."

Rabbit hopped over to the window and looked out with him. He nodded to the left side of the yard, his large ears tapping at the window. "The snow is already starting to melt," Rabbit said. "I'm sure Mayor Kligore wants to make sure the snow is gone as soon as possible. If he was behind today's terror, then he probably has some reason to hate the snow."

"I don't understand how one man can have so much power," Harry said.

"His power is temporary, Harry. And not as strong as he likes to think."

148

Harry thought of how Declan had looked after the snowball fight with his busted lip and slightly swollen face. He thought of all the tears he had seen on the faces of small children today. *Sure seems pretty powerful to me,* Harry thought.

"Were you there today?" Harry asked.

"Of course I was."

"Did you see what Titus did? He saved me from getting clobbered. If his dad found out, that could be very bad for him."

"He came through for you because he understood that what he and his brother were doing was wrong," Rabbit said. "In the end, his thing behind the thing was not as important as doing what was right."

"The thing behind the thing," Harry said. "You mean wanting to make his dad happy?"

"Perhaps," Rabbit said.

"Do I have a thing behind the thing?" Harry asked.

"Well, if your thing is helping those in need or those that can't defend themselves, then I think your thing *behind* the thing is pretty obvious."

"The Good Magic," Harry said. "The Great Magician."

Rabbit nodded and hopped back over toward the bed. "And did you notice, Harry? You won today. You did the right thing and stood up for those kids. You were victorious, and you didn't even have to use magic."

"I did notice that," Harry said, looking at his desk where his backpack and wand were sitting.

Rabbit smiled. "Good night, Harry."

"Goodnight."

Harry continued to stare out of the window, noticing that the snow on the roof was starting to melt and drip down into the gutters. He then thought of something Samson had said about the snow earlier that day.

It covers the ugly.

Maybe that was why Mayor Kligore didn't like it. Maybe the snow was too much like a blank canvas. Maybe it was too much like beauty or hope.

To the right of Harry's window, headlights crept along the road. Harry watched as the snowplow came meandering down the road, striking the curb and swerving to right itself. He

smiled, took one last glance at the snow, and returned to bed.

That night, when he dreamed of sledding down Haunted Hill, there were no Four Snowmen of the Snowpocalypse or twisted ankles. There was only white and more white as far as the eye could see.

There were no bullies, no injuries, no danger. The snow was perfect and unbroken, forever covering the ugly in all directions.

152

MARK ANDREW POE

Harry Moon author Mark Andrew Poe never thought about being a children's writer growing up. His dream was to love and care for animals, specifically his friends in the rabbit community.

153

Along the way, Mark became successful in all sorts of interesting careers. He entered the print and publishing world as a young man, and his company did really, really well.

Mark became a popular and nationally sought-after health care advocate for the care and well-being of rabbits.

Years ago, Mark came up with the idea of a story about a young man with a special connection to a world of magic, all revealed through a remarkable rabbit friend. Mark worked on his idea for several years before building a collaborative creative team to help bring his idea to life. And Harry Moon was born.

In 2014, Mark began a multi-book print series project intended to launch *The Adventures of Harry Moon* into the youth marketplace as a hero defined by a love for a magic where love and 'DO NO EVIL' live. Today, Mark continues to work on the many stories of Harry Moon. He lives in suburban Chicago with his wife and his twenty-five rabbits.

BE SURE TO READ THE CONTINUING AND AMAZING ADVENTURES OF HARRY MOON

Harry Moon's
DNA

Helps his fellow schoolmates
Makes friends with those who had once been his enemies
Respects nature
Honors his body
Does not categorize people too quickly
Seeks wisdom from adults
Guides the young
Controls his passions
Is curious
Understands that life will have trouble and accepts it
And, of course, loves his mom!

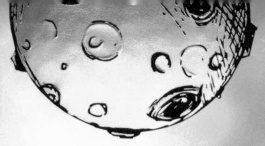

POSTER INSIDE!

HARRY MOON

FIRST LIGHT

MARK ANDREW POE

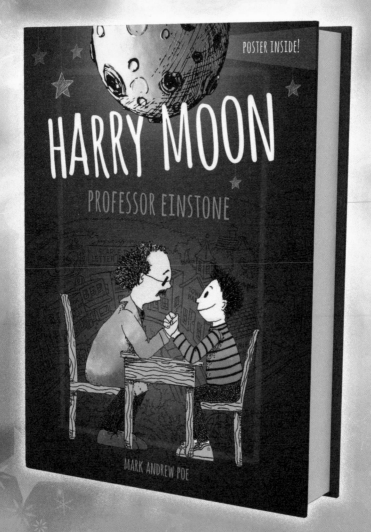

POSTER INSIDE!

HARRY MOON

PROFESSOR EINSTONE

MARK ANDREW POE

POSTER INSIDE!

HARRY MOON

ORIGIN

WAND-PAPER-SCISSORS

MARK ANDREW POE

POSTER INSIDE!

HARRY MOON

HARRY'S CHRISTMAS CAROL

MARK ANDREW POE

FOR MORE BOOKS
& RESOURCES GO TO
HARRYMOON.COM

Honey Moon's
DNA

Builds friendships that matter
Goes where she is needed
Helps fellow classmates
Speaks Her mind
Honors her body
Does not categorize others
Loves to have a blast
Seeks wisdom from adults
Desires to be brave
Sparkles away
And, of course, loves her mom

168

Never Go Alone!

A Sleepy Hollow Spine Tingler

No one ever dared to go into the old Poe mansion on the outskirts of Sleepy Hollow alone. The ancient house was over a hundred years old and rumored to be filled with traps and the most awful of things. Just riding your bike down the sidewalk in front of the sinister property would curl your hair as the sound of an occasional scream or whimper coming from the mansion would cause you to pedal faster.

It was also true that twice a year scouts from the Mummy Mates and the Ghost Brigade Clubs would spend one entire night in the house to earn their Facing-Your-Fear Badges. Nothing in Sleepy Hollow was more terrifying.

The house was ginormously huge with four roofs and three chimneys. Every so often, a stone from one of its walls would clatter to the ground with a crash. The porch railing that wrapped all the way around the house was missing spindles. It looked like a big, scary toothless grin.

Still, some of the kids of Sleepy Hollow liked to challenge each other to at least *walk* past the old manse—if they dared. Most trotted over to the other side of the street.

On this day, Harry Moon chose to walk alone on Shocky Rock Street, the road that ran right past the Poe mansion. The snow from Sleepy Hollow's unexpected snow storm had already melted away. The town was returning to normal. Harry noticed that a wide ribbon of snow and ice drifted around the foundation of the house. "That's wierd," he said out loud. "I wonder why that snow hasn't melted." He investigated.

He stood still for a minute or two looking at

the house. It seemed kind of normal. Well, normal for a Sleepy Hollow spooky house—except for the gleaming, sparkling, white snow piled *around* the foundation. There were even patches of the white stuff in the yard and glistening snow still hugged some tree trunks. It was like the snow had forgotten to melt at just this one street address.

Harry patted his back pocket. He wanted to make certain his trusty magic wand was there, just in case he encountered something unexpected. Then he stepped off the curb and walked across the street. As he walked closer he thought he heard a sound, a weird noise, coming from the house.

But this was something he had never heard before. Or at least he couldn't remember ever hearing such a woeful, deep, grinding soulless sound.

With his wand now grasped firmly in his hand, Harry stopped walking and listened again. Yes, it was definitely an awful sound, and it was definitely coming from the Poe house.

He swallowed hard and stepped deliberately toward the house. He pushed open the gate of the long wrought-iron fence that surrounded the property. The fence was pretty amazing itself—black with small iron ravens on each post. Eerie iron vines snaked their way around the entire fence.

Harry took another step and stopped. He waited with ears perked, listening for the sound and—SCREEEEEECCCCCCCHHHHHHHHHHHH!!!! There it was. Only louder and more desperate and soulless than he had heard from across the street.

Harry swallowed again. He pointed Wand toward the house. He took another step and stopped cold, paralyzed by another sound. A softer, different sound. He was surrounded. Harry's heart thumped in his ears. Was it a ghost?

"Who is that?" Harry called. "Who's there?"

Harry spun around on one foot. He raised his wand in the air and shouted, "ABRA—" and stopped. It was Rabbit.

"Oh, c'mon, it's you," Harry said. "You scared the bejeebers out of me."

"Yeah, I have that effect on some people."

"Aww, Rabbit," Harry said. "Is this all you? Are

you making that awful noise? Are you *trying* to scare me?"

Rabbit pulled his ears down and rolled his eyes. "Me? No. I was just wondering why you were here, alone. No one comes to Poe House *alone*."

"I . . . I noticed the snow—it's leftover from that wacky storm. It's melted everywhere else in town but here. I wanted to investigate."

"Uhmm, yes, that is strange. And come to think of it—it's much colder here than at your house."

173

"Should we investigate?"

Just then the sound came louder and louder. More desperate.

SCCCCCRRRRREEEEEEEEEEEECCCCHHHHHHHHH!!

Harry jumped back, nearly toppling over Rabbit. Fortunately, Rabbit moved fast and hopped out of the way. "Watch yourself, Harry."

"Sorry, Rabbit, maybe I should just go home."

"Uhmm, maybe," Rabbit said. "But aren't you

curious?"

"Well, sure, but you know what they say about curiosity."

"But I'm a rabbit, not a cat, although—LOOK!"

Harry whirled and saw, slinking across the lawn, a large black cat. It stopped for a moment, its green eyes glistening in the cold, and looked straight at Harry. Harry could feel the cat's stare penetrate his brain. He shook the feeling away.

"C'mon, it's just a cat," Harry said. "I'm going home."

"Suit yourself," Rabbit said. "But I'd sure like to know why the snow hasn't melted here. And what is that awful sound?"

SCCCCCRRRRREEEEEEEEEEECCCCHHHHHHHHH!!

"I don't know," Harry said, "and I'm not sticking around to find out."

Harry ran all the way home. He was never so happy to step foot in his kitchen. Mary Moon was there stirring soup on the stove and grilled cheese sandwiches crackled on the griddle.

"H-h-hey, Mom," Harry said. He wrapped his arms around her waist and hugged her so hard she nearly lost her balance.

"Hi, Harry," she said. "You okay?"

"Sure, Mom, just glad to see you. It was a weirdly long day."

Mary tapped the wooden spoon against the pot. "Something happen?"

"Not really. Just school and kid stuff. You know."

"Yeah, I know. Now sit down. Dinner's ready. Call your sister first."

"HONEY! Dinner's ready!"

Mary Moon shook her head. "Harrold. I could have done that."

But it worked because just as Mary Moon set bowls of minestrone on the table Honey appeared.

"Dad's working late," Mary Moon said. "So it's just us tonight. Harvest had a stomachache so he's sleeping."

"Ewww," Honey said, "did he puke?"

"Honey," Mary said, "not while we're eating, but yes, he did."

Harry swallowed and held his stomach. Yuck. "Gross."

"Good soup," Honey said.

Harry just pushed the vegetables swimming in the broth around. All he could see was Harvest throwing up.

"Uh oh," Mary Moon said. "You okay, Harry? You're not eating. You aren't getting sick are you?"

Harry smiled. "Oh, no, I'm fine, Mom, just thinking."

"All right then, eat. You'll feel better."

After dinner, Harry went to Honey's room where she was studying.

"Hey," Honey said, "what gives? You never come in here."

"Listen," Harry said. He stopped and closed the door behind him quietly. "I have to tell you something."

Honey closed her social studies book and sat up straight. "Ooooo, I'm listening. Are you gonna do some magic on Kligore?"

Harry shook his head. "No, no, this is different. Now listen."

Then Harry told Honey all about the snow at Poe House and the strange sounds and even about the cat.

Honey laughed. "Oh, Harry, Harry, you're such a numbskull. Old houses make noise all the time." She shivered.

"Nah," Harry said. "I've heard those old house creaks and rattles too. This is different. And what about the snow? How come it never melted?"

Honey pushed some stray hairs out of her eyes. "Hmm, that one is weird. Whatcha gonna do? Investigate?"

Harry nodded. "Yeah, you and me?"

"Me?" Honey said. "Why not your Good Mischief Twerps?"

"Team," Harry said, with a frown. "It's the Good Mischief Team."

Honey smiled. She loved to get Harry's goat every chance she could.

Harry grabbed Honey's coat from her desk chair and tossed it to her. "You comin' or not?"

Honey zipped her jacket. "Awww, big brother a 'fraidy cat? He need his little sister to protect him? What about your crazy wabbit?"

"Knock it off, Honey. I just think it will be better if we both go."

Honey swallowed. She looked through her window. She became serious. "But it's dark out there. I don't think Mom will like this."

"Awww, who's the 'fraidy cat now?"

Honey folded her arms across her chest. "Not me. Let's go."

"Grab a flashlight," Harry said.

Harry and Honey walked quickly toward Poe House. But when they turned onto Shocky Rock Street, they slowed their pace. Not that they decided to slow down together. It just kind of happened.

"Okay," Harry said, "almost there. Flashlight?"

Honey turned on the flashlight. "Check."

"Cell phone?" Harry said.

Honey touched her pocket. "Check."

They crept closer to the mansion.

"Wand?" Honey asked.

Harry felt his back pocket. "Absolutely."

They walked one more block and there stood the Poe mansion, more imposing than ever at night, illuminated only by the streetlights—streetlights that sometimes blinked off for no reason. Harry figured it was one of Kligore's tricks to make Sleepy Hollow seem more spooky and unpredictable. He silently hoped that wouldn't be the case tonight.

Harry and Honey now stood directly across the street from the creepy, ancient house.

"Okay," Harry said. "This is it."

"But I don't hear anything." Honey whispered.

"Oh, you will." At least, Harry hoped. How stupid would he feel if the house never made the sound again or worse, what if it only made the sound when he was there—alone.

But just as they stepped off the curb into the black street, the night air was blasted.

SCCCCCCCCCRRRRRRRREEEEEEEEEEEEEC-CCCCCCCCCCHHHHHH!

Honey grabbed Harry's arm. "I heard that! What is it?"

"I don't know," Harry said. "Come on."

They walked closer and closer and closer to the house. In the night sky, the clouds moved away

from the full moon almost on cue, as though someone had willed it. Snow, piled around the tree trunks, sparkled in the moonlight.

"That is really weird," Honey said. "The sssnnnnoooow, I mean."

SCCCCCCCCRRRRRRREEEEEEEEEEEEC-CCCCCCCCCCHHHHHH!

"Wow, there it is again," Honey said. "That's nuts!"

181

"Are you scared?" Harry asked.

"Of course," Honey said. "Let's go."

Harry stepped onto the porch first. The sagging wood creaked under his feet.

"That's not the same sound," Honey said.

"Sure isn't," Harry said. "We have to go inside."

They crept closer to the front door, and just as Harry was about to grab the knob, a mighty wind enveloped them and pushed the door open with a BANG!

"Are you really sure you want to do this?" Harry asked. Honey was now clinging to him like a vine on a fence.

"We have to do this," Honey said as she let go. "Let's stay close to each other."

"Come on. Turn on your flashlight."

SCCCCCCCCCRRRRRRRREEEEEEEEEEEEC-CCCCCCCCCCHHHHHH!

"It's getting louder now," Harry said. "It's coming from over there. Toward the old kitchen."

"Okay," Honey said. "Let's go."

SCCCCCCCCCRRRRRRRREEEEEEEEEEEEC-CCCCCCCCCCHHHHHH!

Honey swallowed, the flashlight shaking in her hand. She shined her light into the kitchen. "What's that?" she asked. "It looks like, like a monster."

Harry shined his light on the spot. "Nope. Just some old clothes and boxes."

SCCCCCCCCCRRRRRRRREEEEEEEEEEEEC-

CCCCCCCCCCHHHHHH!

Honey and Harry moved closer to the pile. They heard the sound, but it was now dimmer and softer.

"Rabbit?" Harry called. "Is that you? Playing tricks again?"

Nothing. Not a sound. They stepped closer.

Honey pulled a large overcoat from the pile and jumped back. "Oh great googly ghosts!" she hollered.

183

"What is it?" Harry shined his light, and there, under the pile of clothes, was the large black cat he had seen earlier.

"It's just a cat," Honey said as if asking a question.

"Can't be," Harry said. He moved more clothing aside. Snuggled in the rubble was a litter of kittens, mewing and meowing and pawing at the big black cat.

"Oh, look," Honey said. "It's kitties! They're soooooo cute. We need to bring them home.

They're probably *freez*—"

SCCCCCCCCRRRRRRREEEEEEEEEEEEC-
CCCCCCCCCHHHHHH!

Honey shivered. Harry grasped his wand and pointed his flashlight toward a door in the kitchen. "It's coming from . . . from the basement."

"Come on," Honey said. "We have to check it out." She placed the overcoat over the kittens. "Stay warm. We'll be back—"

SCCCCCCCCRRRRRRREEEEEEEEEEEEC-
CCCCCCCCCHHHHHH!

"I hope!"

Harry pushed open the basement door. "It's down there. Whatever it is."

Harry took Honey's hand, and they walked down the rickety steps one slow step at a time. The were many noises now, some low and deep, some high and screeching.

Harry stepped onto the basement floor and shined his light around. "Holy cow, it stinks down here. Gag."

"Yeah," Honey said, "like mildew mixed with Harvest's puke mixed with your farts."

Harry grunted. "Okay, okay."

They made their way across the dark basement. Harry shined his light on the crumbling stucco wall. "What's that?"

Large splotches and small rivers of wetness covered the wall.

"IT'S BLOOD!" Honey screamed.

"No, it's not," Harry said.

S C C C C C C C R R R R R R - REEEEEEEEEEEECCCCCCCCCCCHHHHHH!

SCCCCCCCCRRRRRRRREEEEEEEEEEEEC- CCCCCCCCCHHHHHH!

"It's getting louder," Harry said.

"I'm scared," Honey said. "It's getting closer too. It's going to eat us!"

Harry shined his light at the old iron pipes crisscrossing the ceiling like silly string. His light landed on a large pipe.

"Look," Harry said. "It's . . . It's gonna blow!"

SCCCCCCCCRRRRRRREEEEEEEEEEEEC-
CCCCCCCCCHHHHHH!

And blow it did! The pipe burst and water rained down onto the basement and onto Harry and Honey. The other pipes were grunting and groaning and shaking. Harry hollered, "Run! The ceiling is falling!" He grabbed Honey's hand, and they dashed up the steps just in time for one final ear-splitting SCCCCCCCCCRRRRRRRREEEEEEEEEEEECCCC-CCCCCCHHHHHH!

"Pipes!" Harry said. "It was the water pipes all along! We have to get out of here!"

"We have to get the cats!" Honey yelled. She reached the top of the stairs and ran toward the kittens. She managed to snuggle all six kittens inside her jacket. She held the tired mama cat in her arms. "You're coming with us!"

She took a step and then froze. Something even more terrible was happening.

"Don't move!" Harry screamed. "The floor. It's

gonna buckle away under you."

Tears streamed down Honey's cheeks. "What should I do?"

"Stand perfectly still."

SCCCCCCCCRRRRRRRREEEEEEEEEEEEC-CCCCCCCCCCHHHHHH!

BLAM!

"Pipes are bursting all over the house. The whole house is gonna blow!" Harry said.

187

Honey pushed her tears away. "I'll cry later," she said. "Harry. This calls for—"

"Good Magic," Harry said. He pulled his wand from his pocket. He raised it high.
"Walls and floors,
Doors and pipes,
Come to order!
ABRACADABRA!"

SCCCCCCCCRRRRRRRREEEEEEEEEEEEC-CCCCCCCCCCHHHHHH!

"Harry, it's not working!" Honey cried.

Harry took a deep, deep breath and shook his wand.

"Walls and floors,
Doors and pipes,
Fall back together!"

This time the screeching stopped. The floors stopped buckling. The house gave up a loud sigh, like it was tired and wanted to sleep. A coldness seemed to rush out the front door, and the house, in an instant, returned to its original self—strong and healthy.

Harry grabbed Honey's hand. "I don't know how long that will keep. Let's scram."

They dashed out of the house—Honey still held the kittens and mama cat.

They ran to the end of the Poe house walkway, shivering against the cold.

"We made it," Honey said. "We made it."

Harry looked at the house that, at least for that moment, looked brand new. "It's beautiful," he said. "A real masterpiece."

"Yeah," Honey said. "Too bad no one cared enough to keep it in good repair."

But just as emergency car headlights with lights flashing pulled onto the property, the house fell back into its awful, scary self. A side wall crumbled nearly to dust. Flakes of plaster floated in the moonlight like snow.

The car stopped. It was Officer Ortiz. "There you are," the officer called. "Your folks are worried sick. What in the world is happening here? The neighbors are calling the station."

189

"Sorry," Harry said. "We were just . . ."

"I wanted to rescue these kittens," Honey said.

Officer Ortiz shook his head. "Foolish thing to do. You could have been killed. I've called for backup to tape off the property. No one is going back into that house."

Later that night, after they had dried off and changed into their pajamas, Harry and Honey explained the whole thing to their parents.

"I still don't get why there was still snow around the old house," Harry said.

Harry's dad sipped his hot chocolate and said, "It's what happens, Harry. The house was cold. Unloved. The snow stuck around because of that, I suppose. And that's why the pipes burst. It was just so cold."

Honey looked over at the makeshift kitty nursery she and her mom had made—a large box filled with old towels. The kittens mewed loudly, but it was certainly not a scary sound.

"Even in the coldest places we can still find some warmth," she said.

Mary Moon smiled and hugged Honey. "It was a brave thing you did. Brave and reckless. You know tomorrow we'll take the kittens and their mother to the shelter."

"I know," Honey said. "I know."